THE INCREDIBLE HULK

...credible Hulk, the Movie © 2008 MVL Film Finance LLC. Marvel, ...lulk, all character names, and their distinctive likenesses: TM & © 20... Marvel Entertainment, Inc. and its subsidiaries.

...ieate and printed in England by Clays Ltd, St Ives plc

Adapted by
J. E. BRIGHT

Based on the screenplay by
ZAK PENN
and EDWARD NORTON

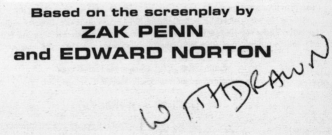

WITHDRAWN

PUFFIN BOOKS

Published by the Penguin Group
Penguin Books Ltd, 80 Strand, London WC2R 0RL, England
Penguin Group (USA) Inc., 375 Hudson Street, New York, New York 10014, USA
Penguin Group (Canada), 90 Eglinton Avenue East, Suite 700, Toronto, Ontario, Canada M4P 2Y3
(a division of Pearson Penguin Canada Inc.)
Penguin Ireland, 25 St Stephen's Green, Dublin 2, Ireland (a division of Penguin Books Ltd)
Penguin Group (Australia), 250 Camberwell Road, Camberwell, Victoria 3124, Australia
(a division of Pearson Australia Group Pty Ltd)
Penguin Books India Pvt Ltd, 11 Community Centre, Panchsheel Park, New Delhi – 110 017, India
Penguin Group (NZ), 67 Apollo Drive, Rosedale, North Shore 0632, New Zealand
(a division of Pearson New Zealand Ltd)

PROLOGUE

The cold wind whistled across an icy road through the Alaskan tundra. Only one vehicle crept along the road: an oil tanker truck, navigating the high pass. When the truck reached a plateau, the occupants could see mountains and glaciers in the distance, and, further out, the edge of the greenish North Sea.

The driver glanced at his passenger, a quiet, bearded hitch-hiker with haunting eyes. When the passenger looked back, the driver nodded and slowed the truck down to a stop.

The man climbed out of the truck's cab, pulled his backpack on to his shoulders, and raised the hood of his parka. Then he strode towards the mountains. He trudged across the snowy fields. It took him several hours to reach the base of the glacier and he was already chilled to the bone when he began to climb the jagged wall of ice.

As night fell, he lost track of how long he'd been walking. He was so cold that he couldn't feel his body. Finally, with the colourful sheets of the aurora borealis shimmering above, he stopped to stare at the immensity of the dark green sea in front of him.

He stared out blankly from his watering eyes. He flinched as a painful memory struck him: *A woman's body slumped on the floor. A gash bled from her forehead. Crushed lab equipment on top of two people beside her –*

After the experiment had gone so wrong, he had done unforgivable things. He was a danger to everyone he'd ever known. The guilt and shame were unbearable.

His heart – instead of slowing as it froze – speeded up. His pulse throbbed in his ears, growing more insistent. At the base of his skull a green glow appeared, eerie in the darkness. With a blink his eyes turned from blue to green.

A bright green flare of light flashed against the snow.

He collapsed face-first towards the ice. His arm shot out to stop his fall, but it had changed. His once pale, slim arm was suddenly huge, throbbing with thick muscles and glowing a dark, cool green. The Hulk had returned.

He howled from the pain and rage, and the deep scream whipped into the wind. A chunk of the glacier cracked off and rumbled down into the sea. The ice sank into the depths of the green water, trailing angry bubbles in its wake.

CHAPTER 1

Five years later Bruce Banner had cleaned himself up. He was far from being at peace with the past, but at least now he had a plan. Bruce had moved to Brazil, keeping a low profile in an overly populated shanty town called Porto Verde.

He ran through the hills around the town, keeping to its fringes, training his heart to beat slowly during punishing exercise.

When he reached the top of a hill, Bruce glanced at the slum below. It was teeming with people, the perfect place to disappear. He checked the pulse monitor on his wrist: ninety beats per minute. That was low for someone running so quickly.

After his workout Bruce headed home through the bustling, narrow streets of the town. Since he'd shaved his beard, he didn't stand out in the throng of Brazilians walking through the colourful market stalls.

Bruce stopped at one stall that accepted foreign mail to see if the package he'd been expecting had arrived. The stall owner ducked behind a curtain to check and returned with a small box. Bruce took his package and continued home.

He was living in a top-floor apartment of a sturdy four-storeyed brick building. It seemed out of place on his block, which was mostly made up of squat shanties with tin roofs.

Bruce entered his apartment and patted his dog on the head. He opened the package and pulled out a book on plants. He carried it over to where his laptop was set up on a roughly constructed desk and pulled up his instant messenger program. When he saw that Mr Blue was online, Bruce sent him a message. Bruce's screen name was Mr Green, for obvious reasons.

> **Mr Green:** Knock, knock. Received your package. Many thanks. The search continues.
> **Mr Blue:** Happy hunting.

Bruce signed off. He picked up a piece of paper from his desk and leaned back in his chair.

On the paper was a grainy printed-out photograph of a gorgeous woman with refined features and long dark hair. The caption read DR ELIZABETH ROSS. Bruce sighed. Betty Ross had been his girlfriend, as well as his lab partner in the experiment that had gone so wrong. He missed her desperately, but he would never let himself be in a position to hurt her again. She didn't know where he was now, and he was going to stay hidden until he solved his problem. Seeing the botany book gave Bruce a twinge of hope.

Bruce ate dinner in front of the TV, and then studied Portuguese, the language of Brazil. Before getting into bed, he closed up his laptop and tucked it and its Internet antenna into his backpack, which he kept by his bed. If the army found him, he was ready to make a clean getaway, leaving no evidence behind.

Bruce sat in quiet meditation for a good hour. He blocked out the sound of a neighbour's dog barking somewhere in the building.

Then, with his dog by his side, Bruce slipped into a peaceful, hopeful slumber.

The next morning Bruce lined up outside the bottling factory where he worked. Next to his Brazilian co-workers, Bruce filed into the bulky building and followed the male labourers into the changing rooms.

The men's locker room was grimy, with a single naked lightbulb overhead. Bruce changed his shirt, ignoring the four rowdy, tough guys shoving one another playfully behind him.

One of the tough guys pushed another one too hard, and the second guy stumbled and knocked into Bruce. Bruce didn't react at all, but it wasn't like the guy was going to apologize anyway. He wasn't the type.

On the factory floor, Bruce lugged a container of bottle caps between rows of steam pipes and conveyor belts to an open area, where he could see the tin roof of the warehouse high above and the rickety-looking catwalks along the edges that led to the tops of the taller machines. Bruce walked alongside the conveyor belt, delivering caps to the workers on the bottling line. The drink they were bottling today had a label that read: AMAZONA SODA WITH GUARANA KICK!

The beans from the Brazilian guarana plant had three times as much caffeine as coffee. He wasn't going to drink any of that soda – not when he was trying to keep his pulse down!

As Bruce moved down the assembly line, a young woman named Martina smiled at him from her labelling station. Bruce smiled back politely.

During his break Bruce took his botany book from his locker and headed out to the delivery bays. There he found a supply driver who did errands in the jungle for a small fee. Bruce showed the driver a specific flower in the book, and the driver nodded and shook his hand.

After work Bruce stopped by the martial-arts studio where he'd been taking *aikido* lessons. Aikido was mostly about body control and defence – how to protect yourself while doing no harm to your attacker. The Japanese instructor had taught Bruce the breathing techniques that were helping him.

While Bruce was working on a passing move, the instructor accidentally scratched Bruce on the arm with his fingernail. The second Bruce saw blood ooze from the scratch, he stopped cold. He wiped up the blood and applied a line of extra-strength adhesive glue to the cut.

On his way home, Bruce checked the piles of garbage on the streets. This habit had helped him find some useful items for the laboratory he was putting together. That day he found an old record player that still turned. At home he used the record player to create a centrifuge, a machine that spun liquids in test-tubes so fast, they separated into layers of different materials.

Bruce practised his breathing techniques, but that night he couldn't find peace. The problem wasn't just the sound of his neighbour's dog barking again. Bruce shuddered, struck with painful flashes of memory.

He opened his eyes, gasping for breath. He was covered with sweat, and he struggled to control his speeding heartbeat. His pulse monitor read eighty-five beats per minute – dangerously high considering he was at rest.

Finally the aikido breathing techniques settled his pulse rate, and Bruce slipped back into deep meditation.

By the time he went to bed, he'd got his pulse down to thirty-seven beats per minute.

CHAPTER 2

The next day Bruce's manager at the bottling plant called him up to a catwalk. Bruce climbed the metal stairs above the conveyor belts that transported filled bottles. The belt had stopped running.

The manager explained in Portuguese that the machine had broken and he asked Bruce to check it. Bruce pulled the metal panel off the switch box and fiddled with the wires. It didn't take him long to fix the problem.

The manager smiled when the bottles underneath the catwalk began to move again on the conveyor belt.

As Bruce replaced the cover on the switch box, he accidentally sliced his thumb on the metal edge. A trickle of blood dropped towards the bottles below.

'Stop!' Bruce yelled. He hit the off button, and the bottles halted. Bruce ran down on to the conveyor belt, desperately searching for the spot where his blood had landed. He stepped among the bottles, hunting, until he found a drop of blood on the side of one bottle.

Bruce sighed with relief and wiped the bottle clean. Then he signalled up to the manager that all was clear.

As Bruce applied extra-strength adhesive glue to his cut, the manager shook his head, amused by Bruce's strange behaviour. Bruce gave him a smile and a shrug.

But Bruce wouldn't have smiled if he'd known that he'd missed a spot of blood . . . a drip that oozed inside the mouth of a bottle as it trundled towards the capping area.

When the final whistle of the day sounded, Bruce headed outside and was excited to see the supply driver waiting for him. Bruce ran over and accepted a small bunch of flowers that the driver had brought. Bruce paid him and hurried home with the rare blossoms from the jungle.

When Bruce got home, he put the flowers down and set up his laptop and Internet link to contact Mr Blue.

> **Mr Green:** I got the plant.
>
> **Mr Blue:** And you have my notes on how to break down its chemicals into the inhibitor formula?
>
> **Mr Green:** Yes.
>
> **Mr Blue:** For most cellular exposures, a concentration of 50–80 parts per million will be enough. Keep me posted. And good luck. :)

Bruce signed off and got to work. Finally, after much painstaking effort, Bruce gathered a small amount of the purplish formula in a test-tube, a formula he hoped would give him back his real life.

After pricking his finger, Bruce squeezed a drop of his blood on to a glass slide. He peered down at the slide through a microscope and adjusted the focus until he could see his blood cells. His red cells were fringed with a light green glow. They'd shown that eerie radiation since his accident back at Culver University five years ago.

Bruce took out the slide. He filled an eyedropper with the purple formula. Then he squeezed out three drops on to his blood on the slide and stuck the slide back under the microscope.

Peering into the eyepiece Bruce saw the purple formula seeping into his blood from the edges. When the purple formula hit the green glow, it hissed and frothed, sizzling around the cells. Bruce lost sight of his cells as the blood seemed to boil, but then the mixture calmed.

All the purple formula had disappeared. His red cells remained the same: surrounded by the glow of green gamma radiation.

The experiment was a failure, and Bruce felt sick with the loss of hope. Eventually Bruce got up from the lab table and went to his laptop to tell Mr Blue the disappointing results.

Mr Green: No lessening of the gamma.

Mr Blue: None? Your tissue exposure to the gamma must have been high. Try a higher concentration of the formula. *Slightly* higher. 100 parts per million=lethal toxicity.

Bruce glanced over at the wilted and shredded flowers on the lab table. He'd milked them dry.

Mr Green: Impossible. Supply is limited.

Mr Blue: Not here. We're making a pure synthetic by the gallon. Send me a blood sample.

Mr Green: That's not a good idea.

Mr Blue: You need help. Gamma is not something to mess with.

'You can say that again,' Bruce mumbled.

He turned around to stare at the squashed flowers behind him. What other options did he have? He got up and began to extract his own blood with a syringe until he had filled a test-tube. Then he labelled the tube MR GREEN and packaged it up.

CHAPTER 3

Bruce was having a nightmare – or a memory. It was hard for him to tell the difference any more.

The hospital room was blinding white behind the glass wall. Betty was hooked up to tubes and life-support machines, unconscious. She looked so small.

A strong hand landed on Bruce's shoulder. He looked up to see General Ross staring at him.

Bruce had never felt so tired in his life, so filled with misery. Worst of all was the rage that lingered in his blood. It was terribly dangerous. 'Three people were hurt,' Bruce told General Ross. 'I don't care about the programme.'

Ross's eyes glared down at him, like brilliant car headlights. 'You're insane,' the general spat out.

Bruce pushed past him, running through the swinging hospital doors, disappearing in a flash of white light . . .

In his Pentagon office, General Ross snapped out of his reverie when Major Kathleen Sparr put a stack of forms on to his desk. Ross signed the forms automatically. They were basic requisition orders, dull and routine.

'Here's something more interesting,' Sparr said. She held out a fax. 'Possible gamma sickness. Milwaukee. A boy drank one of those guarana sodas. It had more kick than he was looking for.'

Ross scanned the fax. 'The last three were irradiated fruit, not gamma.'

Sparr pointed out a chemical composition chart. 'Look at the spectrograph in that report,' she said. 'Whatever that boy drank was *concentrated*. He got less than a tenth of a millilitre, and it almost killed him.'

'Where was the soda bottled?' Ross asked.

Major Sparr checked the fax. 'Porto Verde, Brazil.'

Ross raised his eyebrows. 'Remember that package we tracked to the girl that just had seeds in it?' he asked. 'A year and a half ago, maybe?'

'Orchid seeds,' Sparr replied. 'It came from Brazil.'

Ross banged his hands down. This was his first real lead in years! 'Get our agency people looking for an American at that bottling plant,' he demanded. 'Tell them no contact . . . If he sees them, he's gone. And get me Joe Greller!'

Two hours later a transport van stopped near the runway of a military base. Two special forces soldiers hopped out of the van and hustled over to join three other commandos waiting for them on the tarmac.

They greeted one another gruffly. 'Who's our sixth man?' asked the tallest soldier.

'Blonsky,' a commando with blue eyes replied.

Neither the tall man nor the chunky soldier he'd arrived with recognized the name. 'I've never worked with him,' the tall commando said. 'Is he a rookie?'

The blue-eyed soldier chuckled. 'When Blonsky was a rookie, you were still a baby,' he answered.

The chatter stopped as a helicopter banked in for a landing. Before the chopper was fully at rest, a short, muscular soldier with dirty blond hair leaped out.

'*That's* Blonsky,' the blue-eyed soldier said as they boarded a waiting C-130 transport plane.

General Ross strode out of the operations building at the edge of the tarmac. He was accompanied by Major Sparr and his old friend General Joe Greller.

'I got who I could,' Greller reported to Ross. 'It was short notice, but they're all quality.' He handed over the commandos' personnel files to Sparr. 'I pulled you one ace,' Greller said. 'You'll figure out who.'

'I know you cashed in some chips for this, Joe,' Ross said. 'I'm grateful.'

Greller nodded. 'I was glad to do it,' the general said.

As the plane buzzed towards Brazil, Major Sparr handed out briefing folders containing photos of Bruce Banner, Banner's apartment building and the town of Porto Verde. The commandos studied them.

'This is the target and the location,' Sparr lectured. 'Snatch and grab only. Live capture. You'll have dart clips and suppression weapons. Live fire for back-up only. We've got help from the local authorities, but we want this mission quiet. The only way this will get exciting is if you guys mess it up.'

Ross joined the briefing in the back of the plane. Blonsky looked up at him. 'Is Banner a fighter?' Blonsky asked.

'Your target is a fugitive from the US government who has stolen military secrets,' Ross replied curtly. 'Don't wait to see if he's a fighter – put him to sleep.'

Blonsky nodded.

'Each two-man team will be issued a radiation sensor: a Geiger counter that we will monitor remotely as well,' Ross continued. 'At the first blip, I want to know about it.'

'Did this guy steal plutonium?' one soldier asked.

'Something like that,' Ross replied.

CHAPTER 4

It was Friday afternoon. Bruce carted supplies from conveyor belt to conveyor belt, focused on his job.

As he came round the corner of a machine, Bruce spotted Martina. She was surrounded by the four young tough guys who had been play-fighting in the locker room earlier that week.

One of the guys was obviously the leader of the group. He was dressed a little sharper than the others. As Bruce walked closer to them, he could hear him talking to Martina.

'Why do you act so shy?' he asked her, sounding more pushy than friendly.

Martina glanced up as Bruce approached. He could tell instantly from her expression that she needed help. But Bruce hesitated. It was a bad idea for him to get involved.

The head of the group reached out and stroked Martina's cheek. She backed away, but when she hit a wall and he didn't quit teasing her, Martina shoved him away hard.

The tough-guy leader grabbed her arm.

Despite the danger, Bruce stepped up to the group. 'Is . . . everything okay?' he asked Martina. He gulped as her expression told him that no, everything was *not* okay.

'Get lost, mule,' the leader snapped at Bruce.

Bruce pushed in closer. 'You want some coffee, Martina?' he asked. 'With me?'

The group leader stuck his arm out in front of Bruce. 'I said beat it,' he said with a growl. 'You want a problem?'

Bruce raised his hands. 'No problem,' he said.

'Too late,' the guy said. He shoved Bruce in the chest. His friends muscled in closer to Bruce on all sides.

Bruce's pulse began to race as Martina screamed at them to stop. He glanced down at the pulse monitor on his wrist – it was climbing fast, past seventy-five beats per minute, then seventy-six. 'Okay, listen,' he told them in his broken Portuguese. 'Don't make me hungry. You wouldn't like me when I'm –' Bruce bit his lip, realizing that he'd mixed up a word. 'No, wait . . . that's not right . . .'

The leader took a swing at Bruce's face, but he dodged the blow. Using his aikido training, Bruce sidestepped the force of the attack, and the leader went flying past him, stumbling across the factory floor.

As soon as the leader righted himself, he wiped his hands on the front of his jeans, visibly very angry. He began flailing out at Bruce, but none of his punches landed. Bruce avoided the attacks, ducking and weaving, leaving the tough guy flailing like a fool.

'Hey, cut it out!' the factory manager shouted from the catwalk. 'I've got a supply sitting here collecting bugs! You want me to hire someone else? Get back to work!'

The four friends pushed past, laughing like there was no big deal, but from the looks on their faces, Bruce knew he'd be a fool to be caught alone with them.

As soon as they were gone, Martina let out a big sigh and thanked Bruce. He smiled at her, then got back to work.

That night Bruce was relaxing with his dog at his feet, when his instant messenger program chimed. Bruce hopped out of bed and hurried to his laptop.

> **Mr Blue:** A concentration of 150 ppm cancels out the gamma saturation in your sample. It's incredibly toxic, but it works.
>
> **Mr Green:** Encouraging. But sample is baseline. I have . . . gamma spikes . . .
>
> **Mr Blue:** It isn't possible for a spike to exceed the amount of original exposure to the gamma radiation. What was the exact original exposure?
>
> **Mr Green:** Data not available.

Mr Blue: Toxicity at this level too risky without precision.

Mr Green: Will it cure me?

Mr Blue: Barring new gamma exposure . . . there's a good chance.

Bruce sat back in his chair, feeling stunned from the good news. Now all he had to do was somehow retrieve that data from his original experiment. He grabbed a pen and scribbled on a notepad, 'Get data from Maynard'.

After turning off the computer, Bruce stared for a long while at the picture of Betty. He almost allowed himself to hope that searching for the data might bring him back in contact with her . . . But, no, he'd be putting her in terrible danger.

Before Bruce meditated, he remembered to tear the note off the pad and tucked it into his shirt pocket for safekeeping.

As Bruce sat in the lotus position, controlling his breathing, another burst of memory plagued him, even more vivid than usual.

Bruce tried to remain calm as the experiment began. He could see Betty's worried face peering into the lab from behind the glass shield of the control room. She pressed a button and the silvery disc of the gamma radiation emitter slid into position over his head. Bruce could see his own nervous face reflected in the mirrored surface of the disc.

21

Moments later everything in the lab was an insane blur, seen from ten feet above the ground. The giant was filled with pain and fury, and the screams around him scorched his ears. The laboratory lights swirled and flashed, searing his eyes. He had to make it stop – now!

Then the lab was a wreck. Betty was crumpled on the floor with a gash on her forehead. Two nearby laboratory assistants screamed, crushed under lab equipment. General Ross was in the room, shooting a weapon.

The explosions from the weapon's muzzle were intensely, painfully bright. The creature charged at Ross, and when Ross threw up his arm defensively, the giant yanked it so hard that Ross was flung across the room.

The beast glared down at Ross, whose arm was dislocated, inching across the floor towards Betty's unconscious body. Then it let out a roar that shook the lab.

He rushed towards the wall, smashing out of the building towards freedom –

Bruce opened his eyes, gasping for air. His face glistened with sweat. His pulse monitor was climbing past ninety, hitting ninety-one . . .

With a deep sigh, Bruce gave up on meditating. He needed fresh air, so he went up to the roof of his apartment building. There he stood for the next hour, overlooking the sprawl of the town around him, wishing the experiment had never happened.

CHAPTER 5

As Bruce slept, his dog stretched against his feet. The usual hubbub of the town echoed softly into the apartment, and the dog downstairs kept up his regular barking.

Bruce didn't know that tonight the neighbour's dog wasn't just barking at nothing.

In the shadows of the apartment's back alley, a commando scanned the rear entrance of the apartment building with night-vision goggles. The area was clean, so the commando signalled to the other soldiers.

Five other figures stepped out of the shadows and slunk towards the back door. They were clad in black hoods and carried dart rifles, with back-up MP5 submachine guns slung over their shoulders.

In Bruce's apartment the sound of the neighbour's barking dog suddenly ceased. Bruce's own dog looked up and growled.

Downstairs, the commandos climbed up towards their target, their black boots stepping softly on to the landing past the neighbour's dog. The dog twitched, silenced by a tranquillizer dart. When the soldiers reached Banner's apartment door, Blonsky hand-signalled for one of the commandos to head for the roof's steps. Blonsky then motioned for two of the commandos to approach the door. One soldier dropped to his knees and began to snake a miniature video camera that was attached to a thin rod under the door. The other soldier applied packs of explosive plastique to the hinges and lock. Blonsky stepped back and faced the door, his submachine gun held ready.

The soldier couldn't see any movement on the left side of the apartment on the camera's tiny monitor. He adjusted the camera towards the right, and was startled by the sight of a giant dog's muzzle sniffing the camera. Banner's dog licked the lens, and then returned to the bed.

A man seemed to be lying in the bed, quiet in sleep.

The soldier with the camera held up one finger, and then pointed it to the right, signalling that one person inside was low to the ground.

Blonsky keyed a code into his microphone communicator.

Outside the apartment building, General Ross, Major Sparr and a Brazilian officer supervised the commandos' progress from a black van filled with surveillance equipment. When Sparr received Blonsky's signal, she turned her attention to the monitors, which showed feeds from one of the team's helmet cameras, a cam from the back of the building, and the cam from the soldier on the roof.

'Geiger?' asked Ross.

Each soldier had a Geiger counter affixed to the stock of his dart gun. Sparr checked the readouts. 'Negative,' she replied.

Ross nodded. 'Take him,' he ordered Blonsky.

Boom! The plastique ignited, blowing the door off its hinges.

Blonsky hustled into Banner's apartment, with the other commandos covering him. Blonsky spun right, dropped to his knees, and fired three trank darts at the sleeping form. Each dart hit its target – one dart in Banner's body, and one in each of his legs.

Blonsky slowly approached Banner's bed. He yanked the covers back.

On the pillow was a Styrofoam head, covered with a wig and a baseball cap. Blonsky pulled the covers further, revealing bunched-up pillows on the bed.

Blonsky activated his microphone. 'Target's on the move,' he reported.

CHAPTER 6

With his backpack over his shoulders, Bruce lowered himself with a rope from his kitchen window, down into an air shaft that ran through the centre of his building.

As he descended past the window below, his downstairs neighbour caught sight of him. It was Martina from the factory. Bruce silently shushed her before she could scream.

Up in Banner's apartment, Bruce's dog barked furiously. Blonsky scanned the apartment, looking for other means of escape. Then he saw the rope hanging out of the kitchen window. Blonsky dashed to the sink and hoisted himself up to peer down the air shaft.

The rope swung empty. Blonsky noted that the only ground-floor exit from the shaft led towards an alley. 'He's on the ground, going west,' he reported.

The commando guarding the front of the building instantly ran around to the back. The black command van screeched down the alley towards the rear of the building too.

But Bruce had faked them out. He was in Martina's

apartment, crouched by the door. He nodded at Martina, and she nervously opened her front door and glanced outside. She shook her head; nothing out there.

With no time to even thank her, Bruce fled the apartment and sprinted down the stairs. When he reached the front door, he slipped outside and hustled at a controlled walk down the street, with the hood of his sweatshirt flipped up.

As Bruce hurried past the apartment building's alley, he caught a glimpse of the black van and a black-clad commando guarding it. Unfortunately the commando saw him, too.

Bruce broke into a sprint, turning down the street and into the thick of the town. He threaded through the night-time crowd in the slum. His heart rate was rising, inching up past seventy beats per minute. He was worried about The Hulk. He had to stay calm. Otherwise everyone could be in danger.

Behind him, the commandos were already hot on his trail.

Bruce zipped through alleys, ducking under hanging laundry, leaping over baskets, careening across courtyards. Blonsky and his partner followed close behind, correctly guessing Banner's turns through the catacombs of alleys.

When Bruce reached a paved street with fewer people, he bolted at full speed. He had to stop short when his way ended at a steep hillside overlooking another neighbourhood, with a sheer drop to the houses below. Bruce leaped on to the nearest roof, and ran across the tops of the squat buildings, jumping from one roof to the next. His feet pounded on the rusty tin, and shouts of complaint bellowed up from the occupants inside.

Blonsky and his partner reached the hillside a few seconds later, in time to see Banner jumping from house to house. Blonsky scanned the area, looking for a faster way down. The tallest soldier and the blue-eyed commando arrived, then leaped down to follow Banner across the roofs.

Meanwhile the black van circled around the slum at top speed to catch Banner from the other side of the town. The officers stayed glued to their video monitors, watching the chaotic green-lit images of the chase.

Bruce reached an area thick with laundry, and the flapping sheets almost obscured the edge of a roof. He whipped through the cloth, jumping down to another level of roofs, and his hood was knocked back. He continued to barrel across the tops of the rough homes.

The two commandos following him hit the same patch of clothes-lines, but the tall soldier missed the blind jump. He fell hard, rolled to a standing position, and redirected his route through the alleys, quickly catching up on ground level.

In the van, Sparr pointed to the two dots moving together behind Bruce – the tall soldier and the blue-eyed commando – and to the two dots already ahead of Bruce –

Blonsky and his partner. 'Leader, we're at your ten o'clock,' Sparr reported over the microphone. 'Team Two is pushing target at your four. Move right and you've got him boxed.' She glanced up at Ross. 'Three more moves,' she said with satisfaction. 'Game over.'

Ross just raised an eyebrow. He knew Banner's capabilities better than anyone else on the team. He focused on the radiation monitors, which were still flat at zero.

Bruce reached the end of the residential area and hopped down from the last roof into a party area of bars and late-night clubs. The streets here were bustling with drunken revellers; it would be easier to disappear. He launched himself into the midst of the crowd, turned right, and caught a glimpse of Blonsky dropping down off a roof, too. Blonsky fired a dart, and Bruce felt the wind of it missing him by inches. The dart clanged off a tin wall, and Bruce raced deeper into the throng of partying people.

Blonsky charged after Banner, but bumped into a tight knot of people celebrating that slowed him down.

Bruce checked his pulse monitor: 109 . . . 110. He was in trouble. His pulse was too high, and he was really sweating now. He veered into a dark alley, rushed around a corner, and popped out on to a side street where he almost ran headlong into the opened side door of the black van.

Inside the van, Ross looked up, and for a dizzying

29

moment he locked eyes with Bruce. It was the first time they'd seen each other in five years.

Then Bruce broke into motion again and charged across the street in front of the van, launching into another alley.

'Okay,' Sparr reported to the commandos, 'target is past our mobile unit now and heading zero-nine-zero.'

Bruce lurched through the narrow street, breathing hard. When the alley ended, he took a hard right down a busy, wide street, filled with restaurants. Bruce glanced back to see if anyone was following him, and he slammed right into a group of four guys. Bruce recognized them as the tough guys from the bottling plant. His stomach sank.

The guys were rowdy and looking for a fight . . . And for them, no one better than Bruce could have shown up at that exact moment.

The leader of the group looked angrily at Bruce, and took a wild swing at him.

Bruce dodged the leader's attack by using his well-practised aikido passing move, grabbed the guy's sleeve, and used his own momentum to send him crashing into a pile of stinking trash.

Before his friends could react, Bruce ran for it, scurrying into another side alley.

The leader pulled himself out of the trash, and then he and his friends scrambled to chase Bruce.

At the end of the alleyway, Bruce found himself outside the bottling factory. With little time to think, he raced towards it. Seconds later, the tough guys showed up outside the factory, but Bruce was nowhere to be seen. Then the leader heard the faint sound of rattling metal, and glanced over to see the security chain swinging on the factory's back door. Soon they were headed straight for the factory too.

Meanwhile the commandos were stealthily hunting for Bruce in the streets; they knew he couldn't be far. Blonsky climbed back on to a low-hanging roof and surveyed the town. He spotted one of the tough guys slipping round the factory's back door.

'Target acquired,' Blonsky reported.

CHAPTER 7

In the factory's changing room, Bruce heaved deep breaths, his back against the wall. He listened to the drip of the showers as he tried to lower his pulse rate, slowly easing it down from 103 beats per minute to 101.

A noise on the factory floor startled him, and his pulse jumped to 103 again.

He couldn't stay in the locker room, waiting to be found. He crept out amid the machinery, pausing every few steps to listen for footsteps. He could hear the tough guys whispering, drunkenly following him. Bruce threaded through the banks of bottling machines, getting closer to the far side of the factory where he could see an exit sign dimly glowing green.

When Bruce reached his goal, he pushed gently on the latch and slid out through the door.

The leader was waiting for him. He laughed and shoved Bruce back into the factory. Bruce stumbled backward, and then turned to run, but the other tough guys were standing behind him. They gathered around Bruce and began to shove and kick him against the machines.

'Please,' Bruce begged, 'don't do this.' His pulse hit 110 beats per minute.

The guys shoved Bruce to the middle of the factory. The leader pulled off Bruce's backpack and slapped his face. 'What?' the leader sneered. 'Not so tough now, huh? Try those fancy moves again. Come on, we all want to see.' He gave Bruce a hard push, and Bruce fell back on to a knobby piece of equipment, crying out in agony.

Meanwhile the commandos raced into the factory and heard the sounds of pain and laughter. Blonsky signalled for his men to split up, and he slid on his night-vision goggles. He could see the heat signatures of a cluster of men, glowing neon green in the darkness.

The four guys continued to bully Bruce, with two of them pinning him against a labelling machine.

'Please stop,' cried Bruce. His pulse climbed past 113 beats per minute. 'Me. Angry. Very bad.'

'You bad angry?' the leader replied. 'I bad angry!'

Behind him, Bruce spotted a quick motion in the shadows. A black-clad figure crouched in the dim light. Panic flooded his body, and Bruce's pulse shot up to 125, climbing rapidly to 127.

'Let me go!' he yelled. 'Something really bad is going to

happen!' Bruce warned the leader.

'Yeah,' the leader agreed, 'something bad *is* going to happen.'

A commando's night-vision scope alighted on Banner's face, then dropped to sight on his neck.

Bruce saw a gleaming tranquillizer gun's muzzle, peeking out from the shadows. He lunged to the side, pulling the tough guys with him. The leader punched Bruce in the gut, and Bruce crumpled.

Blonsky fired the trank gun, missing Bruce, but nailing one of the tough guys in the neck.

Bruce gasped as his pulse leaped past 180, jumping to two hundred, his heart throbbing.

Blonsky peered through his night-vision goggles at the cluster of green men. One of the shapes dropped where the trank had hit him; one was already huddled on the floor. Then a strange blast of green light flared. All of the commandos' Geiger counters spiked.

In the van, Ross saw the radiation spike and bolted forward in his chair.

Blonsky ripped off his night-vision goggles, then signalled for the other commandos to hold position. He watched as the tough guys, the two who were still upright, nervously backed away.

'Is target neutral?' Sparr asked over the radio. 'Did we

get a shot?' she asked eagerly.

Blonsky couldn't see clearly what was happening, but it looked like Banner was being twisted into strange shapes. Then Banner let out an anguished scream, and a strange tearing sound filled the factory.

'Shut up!' the leader hissed, and he launched a kick at Bruce's warping body. That was the worst mistake of his life. His foot met something insanely hard. Almost too fast to see, the leader was launched upward by his leg, across the expanse of the factory. His terrified scream was drowned out by an inhuman howl from the growing creature in the shadows.

When the roar faded, everyone in the factory fell silent.

Then, yelling, the remaining bully bolted from the shadows. An enormous, muscular arm reached out after him. The guy was grabbed and squished. The beastly hand dropped him, and he fell like a rag doll.

'Where's the target?' Sparr demanded.

She only got stuttered responses and static in reply.

'Put all your tranks in him!' Ross hollered. 'Now!'

Two of the soldiers advanced towards where the giant lurked between enormous juice tanks. They rapidly fired their tranquillizer darts into the darkness. The projectiles fell to the concrete floor, their needles bent as if they'd hit a wall.

A massive foot stepped out of the shadows and crushed the darts. The beast charged, heaving the bottling tanks out of the way with unbelievable strength. The creature then stomped towards the commandos.

The soldiers whipped out their submachine guns. 'Go live!' one screeched. Bottles exploded around the factory, and the bullets pinged off the roof.

Blonsky and his partner ducked behind a bank of machinery. The body of one commando landed nearby, hitting an on switch. The machinery roared to life, trundling broken bottles down the belt with loud clanks and bright, blinking lights.

Between another set of vast tanks, Blonsky saw that the creature was on the move. His partner opened fire, but the tanks prevented a clear shot.

Blonsky spotted a set of stairs to the catwalks above. He raced for it while his partner backed up two other commandos firing at the creature. It was impossible that the soldiers were missing – they had a clear shot now – but the bullets were missing their target and dropping to the ground.

Up on the catwalk, Blonsky peered down as the creature disappeared into a cloud of steam in an open middle area. His partner pulled a stun grenade off his belt and hurled it into the steam. The soldiers ducked for cover.

The grenade hit something and detonated, rocking the factory. The beast's massive form was outlined by the explosion, but then steam covered him again.

The soldiers waited for the outcome of the blast.

Then the pounding of heavy feet shook the floor. A roar and the sickening sound of tearing steel echoed through the room. Out of the steam a gargantuan metal tank lurched forward, like a gigantic sledge, pushed by the giant. It clipped the supports of the catwalk under Blonsky and smashed into the soldiers on the ground. The commandos screamed as they got caught in the heaving machinery.

In the van the soldiers' cameras blinked off, the monitors turning black. All Sparr and Ross could hear over the microphones was moaning.

General Ross pulled open the van's door and dashed outside.

'Sir, no!' Sparr shouted.

Inside the factory Blonsky sprinted along the catwalk above the creature, looking for a clean shot. He got one when he reached the corner. His bullets raked across the beast's shoulder-blade.

Enraged, the creature spun around, swatting the bullets out of the air with his giant hands.

Blonsky reloaded his weapon, his eyes remaining locked on his target. But then he froze in awe as the beast stepped fully out of the shadows.

He was incredibly muscular, bigger than anything Blonsky had ever seen, rippling with terrifying power.

The creature glared up at him with rage, then snarled and flexed his shoulders, grabbing a forklift and hurling it easily up at Blonsky, like he was throwing a baseball.

Blonsky dived to the side as the machinery crashed into the catwalk where he'd just been standing. The catwalk lurched and Blonsky hung on desperately.

The creature grabbed a steel block of machinery off the assembly line and hurled it. This projectile wasn't aimed at Blonsky. With an earsplitting crash it smashed a gaping hole through the wall of the factory.

Ross had just reached the side of the bottling plant when the wall exploded in front of him. He ducked round a corner for cover, then peered around the edge.

The giant stepped out of the hole, his eyes glinting as he looked around. Then he took off running.

Ross watched, his chest heaving, as the beast barrelled away into the night.

CHAPTER 8

After the factory battle Ross's team searched Banner's apartment. A forensics technician inspected Banner's home-made lab while Sparr rifled through his belongings.

'The stuff in the bottles was basic lab chemicals,' Sparr reported to Ross. 'He was cooking up something, but there's no trace of it. He zeroed the place. Not a scrap of paper. Like he knew we were coming.'

'He didn't know,' Ross replied. 'He's just always ready to leave.'

Then Blonsky entered the apartment, carrying Banner's backpack.

'Tell me that's what I'm hoping it is,' Sparr said. She took the backpack and emptied it, pulling out a laptop. A grainy printout of a picture fell out, and Blonsky picked it up.

'Good-looking for a scientist,' Blonsky said, examining the photo of Betty Ross. 'Banner's girlfriend? Or she's helping him?' he asked them.

General Ross snatched the picture of his daughter out

of Blonsky's hands. '*She* is no longer a factor,' he said. 'We closed that door to him long ago. He's alone. He wants to be alone.' He tapped the laptop. 'But see if he's been talking to anybody.'

Blonsky stepped between Ross and Sparr. 'Forgive me,' he said, 'but does somebody want to talk about what went down in there? Because Banner didn't lose us and he wasn't alone. We had him and something hit us. Something *big*.'

Sparr gestured towards a Brazilian officer. 'Our colonel here says there are rumours about sightings. A farmer says he saw a gorilla going into the jungle.'

'That was no gorilla,' replied Blonsky. 'He was ten feet tall and green . . . or grey. I couldn't tell.'

'I didn't see it,' Sparr said. 'But it sounded like an animal.'

Blonsky laughed. 'That was no animal,' he insisted. 'He threw a forklift, like it was a baseball. It was . . . He was the most . . . *incredible* thing I've ever seen.'

'He's gone,' Ross replied flatly.

'Where?' Blonsky demanded. 'Something like that doesn't just disappear.'

'He's got two thousand miles of jungle to hide in,' Ross said. 'He's gone.'

'If Banner knows what that thing was,' Blonsky swore, 'I'm going to find him and put my foot on his throat and ask him. You can have him after that.'

'The local police are on alert,' said Sparr. 'Banner must have got out when that thing attacked.'

Ross cleared his throat. 'That *was* Banner.'

'You mean he led us to it?' Sparr asked.

'No,' said Ross. 'I mean he . . . was Banner. It wasn't an animal – it was him.'

Blonsky shifted nervously. 'You're going to have to explain that statement.'

'No, I don't,' Ross replied. 'You did your jobs well, both of you. We were undermanned, and that's my fault. I didn't think it would happen again. Get our men on the plane. We're going home.' Then he strode out of Banner's apartment.

Sparr and Blonsky stared after the general, dumbstruck.

Bruce woke to birdsong in the forest with no idea where he was. His clothes were in tatters. Groaning, he followed a muddy road out of the woods until he reached a paved highway cutting through the mountains.

Bruce waved down a truck and leaned in the passenger-side window. 'Can you help me?' he asked the driver in Portuguese.

'*No hablo portugués,*' the driver replied.

Bruce realized he was no longer in Brazil. They were in Paraguay, about fifty miles from the Brazilian border. The driver agreed to take Bruce to the nearest town.

Once they got to a village, Bruce found some cheap new clothes at a stall in the market. He got changed in a muddy alley, and was crumpling up his shredded clothes when a piece of paper fell out of his torn shirt.

He grabbed it. It read 'Get data from Maynard'.

Bruce suddenly remembered his plan.

On the C-130 transport plane heading back to the United States, Sparr read through Banner's instant messages with Mr Blue on her laptop while Ross read printouts beside her. He wasn't much of a computer guy. The more Ross read of Banner's attempts to cure himself, the more he shifted uncomfortably in his chair.

'He's trying to get rid of it,' he muttered.

'Get rid of what?' Sparr asked, looking up from her laptop.

'*It*,' Ross replied. 'His chemistry. He's trying to neutralize whatever powers the transformation inside him.'

'And that's not a good thing?' said Sparr.

'No, it's not a good thing, Major,' Ross snapped. 'I'm not after Banner – I want what's inside him!'

With a nod, Sparr changed the subject. 'Well, he's tight, this one,' she said. 'We can't trace where his e-mail went or came from. We'll have the agency people keep their radar up.'

'It doesn't matter,' said Ross grumpily. 'Banner's already on the move.'

CHAPTER 9

Bruce headed towards the United States border using any means of transportation he could find. He rode in the backs of trucks with migrant workers; climbed through hilly, rugged terrain to avoid South American border crossings; and hitch-hiked whenever he could. When he couldn't find a ride, he grabbed some sleep – mostly outdoors or in the doorways of locked stores in small towns.

It took a long time for Bruce to travel through Central America and Mexico, but he finally reached the border of Texas. He crossed at night with a family of Mexican illegal immigrants, helping their kids cross the rocky desert.

Then he hitch-hiked towards the East Coast, keeping to the smaller highways.

General Ross needed major military resources to locate and capture Banner, so he went to his old friend General Greller. In his office Greller listened open-mouthed to Ross's story about what had happened in Brazil.

'You want to tell me that one more time?' Greller asked with disbelief.

Ross stared at his friend squarely. 'Do I look like I'm not being serious, Joe?'

Greller sighed. 'I've known you a long time,' he replied, 'and I've never seen a cooler head under fire. I know something bit you hard down there, but that is one unbelievable white whale story.'

'Ask Blonsky,' Ross suggested.

Blonsky waited outside Greller's office. Ross opened the door and Blonsky followed him inside.

Standing in front of Greller's desk, Blonsky confirmed Ross's story. 'Yes, sir,' he explained. 'I'd say the creature was nine or ten feet tall. I'd put him at fifteen hundred pounds easily, but could've been more. And he was green. I put three clips in him, sir, and he didn't even flinch. I didn't miss – I'd stake my medals on that.'

Greller rubbed his forehead, staring at Blonsky standing at full attention. 'Relax, will you, Blonsky?' he demanded. Then he faced Ross. 'You want to tell me what is really going on here?'

'Banner's work was a tangent of Bio-Tech,' Ross said.

Greller narrowed his eyes. 'You told me you were going to Brazil to nab a scientist,' he said. 'This is another of your super-soldier experiments gone haywire?'

Ross slowly nodded.

Greller groaned. 'Did anything in that programme *not* turn into a mess?'

'Joe,' Ross replied carefully, 'this is something that could be an incredibly dangerous weapon. We have no idea what Banner's intentions are.'

'Put together a new list,' Greller said, sighing wearily. 'And be prepared to explain everything on it!'

Blonsky strode beside Ross down the hall, boiling with curiosity. 'Are you telling me that Banner becomes that thing *at will*?'

'I don't have an answer to that, soldier,' Ross replied.

'Well,' Blonsky persisted, 'if we developed it, how'd it end up in some egghead?'

Ross stopped short. 'You're asking questions above your pay grade, Captain.'

Blonsky ignored him. 'Listen,' he said, 'I've run into bad surprises on missions, and I've seen good guys go down because we didn't know what we were walking into. But this is a whole new level of weird. So when you take another crack at him, I want in. You should be looking for a team that's prepped, because if that thing shows up, tough guys will be crying like babies.'

Ross stared at Blonsky for a long moment, and then a smile twitched on his lips. 'Well,' he said, 'all right, then.'

Ross led Blonsky to a military hangar where they could talk privately among the dark shapes of helicopters. Ross flipped a light on at a roughly constructed mechanic's table and motioned for Blonsky to sit in the single chair.

Pacing as he talked, Ross said, 'What I'm about to share with you is tremendously sensitive to both me, personally, and to the army. You may be aware that we've got an infantry weapons development programme . . . Well, in World War Two, they began a subprogramme for Bio-Tech Force Enhancement.'

'Super soldiers,' said Blonsky.

Ross leaned against a helicopter. 'That's an oversimplification,' he replied, 'but yes. Other research groups try to arm you better, but we were trying to make you better. Banner's work was in a very early phase. It wasn't even a weapons application.

'His team was combining concentrated myostatin with low-dose gamma bursts. He thought they could strengthen cellular resistance to radiation weapons. But our money was running out. Banner was so sure of what he was on to that he tested it on himself. And I let him. It was supposed to be a very low exposure, but something went very wrong.' Ross tapped his lips. 'Or it went very right . . . I still don't know.'

'Why did he rabbit on you?' Blonsky asked.

'Banner is brilliant,' Ross answered, 'but he's a scientist.

He's not one of us. As far as I'm concerned, that man's whole body is property of the US Army.'

Blonsky shifted. 'You were trying other things, too?'

Ross nodded. 'One serum we developed was promising, but it didn't pan out. Or it *did* . . . but it was . . . unstable. I wanted to refine it, but Congress lost their nerve.'

'I have real contempt for people like that,' Blonsky said.

'You and me both,' Ross replied. 'How old are you now, Captain? Forty-five?'

'Thirty-nine,' Blonsky corrected.

'Being out there takes a toll,' Ross said. 'So get out of the field. Get a desk job. You should be a colonel by now.'

Blonsky shook his head. 'I'm a fighter,' he said. 'That's all I ever wanted to be. I'll do it for as long as I can.' He paused, choosing his next words carefully. 'It's funny,' he whispered. 'If I could put what I know now into my body ten years ago . . . that would be a guy I wouldn't want to fight.'

Ross stepped closer. 'I could probably arrange something like that,' he said, 'if you're really interested.'

Blonsky held Ross's gaze. 'You kept some of it.'

'You ever hear of saving for a rainy day?' Ross replied. 'Well, I think it's raining.'

General Ross picked up the serum from the secured medical storage rooms in the basement and took it upstairs to the lab, where two medical technicians were prepping Blonsky for the procedure. They hooked him up to long tubes while the soldier lay on a white table. Ross handed the canister to an assistant.

'You'll get two separate infusions, dripped in very slowly,' the technician explained to Blonsky. 'One deep into the muscle, one into the centre of your bone marrow.' The tech smiled grimly. 'The bone ones are going to hurt.'

Ross put his hand on Blonsky's shoulder. 'You're getting a very low dose,' he said. 'I need you sharp out there. First sign of any side effects and you're off the team until you straighten out. Agreed?'

Blonsky nodded, committed to the path he'd chosen.

Bruce arrived at the sprawling Culver University campus where he used to work. After so long out of the country, a commonplace sight like the campus looked surprisingly foreign to him.

He strode over to a big stone building – the Maynard Hall of Physical Sciences – and watched the students and faculty enter and exit the hall. During a quiet moment Bruce climbed up the stairs and peered through the door's window.

In the lobby was a security checkpoint, with a metal detector and a guard. Bruce knew he shouldn't be heading that way at all.

The security in the hallways and rooms of the building was more lax. On a directory board, he found a listing for 'Cellular Biology – Dr Elizabeth Ross'. Just seeing her name gave him chills, and Bruce hurried outside again.

He didn't go far. He sat on a bench outside the biology building, waiting.

Finally two women walked out.

Bruce froze as he got his first look at Betty Ross in five years. She appeared as beautiful as he remembered, although her dark hair was longer, and a fringe covered her forehead.

He watched as Betty got coffee with her friend from a mobile cart. The women sat at a small table in the sunshine, then said goodbye after their break was over.

Bruce had an overwhelming urge to run to her, but before he could move, a man approached her with a smile. Betty smiled back, and they embraced. Bruce felt like he'd been punched in the stomach as they linked arms and walked away together.

Bruce walked to the edge of campus, and was glad to see that Stanley's Pizza Parlour was still in business. Stan, a thickset man in his early sixties, was an old friend. Just as Stan flipped over the sign on the door to CLOSED, Bruce knocked. Stan jumped, like he'd seen a ghost, then opened the door.

The two old friends settled down to catch up at a table in a private back room.

'There've been so many rumors –' Stan started.

Bruce smiled. 'Stan, I promise you,' he said, 'whatever you've heard isn't true.'

Stan patted Bruce's leg. 'Oh, I know it. But you know how I felt about you two . . . Have you talked to –'

'No,' Bruce replied, ducking his head sadly. 'She's with –'

'His name's Leonard Samson,' Stan supplied. 'He's a head shrink. They say one of the best. But a good guy. Reminds me of you a little . . . Sorry.' Stan clapped his hands once, changing the subject. 'Bruce, what can I do to help you?'

'I could use a place to stay for a few nights,' Bruce said.

Stan opened his arms wide. 'You'll stay in the spare room upstairs. Use the back door – nobody'll see you come or go.'

'Great,' Bruce said. 'One other thing . . . Can I deliver a few pizzas?'

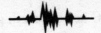

The next evening Bruce set off on a bicycle, dressed in a Stanley's Pizza Parlour uniform, which included a T-shirt, hat and sunglasses. After a few stops to deliver pizzas, he biked over to Maynard Hall and carried two pizzas up to the muscular guard at the lobby's security desk.

'I got a delivery on five,' Bruce told the guard.

The guard looked confused. 'I don't think anyone's up there.'

Bruce let out a groan. 'Oh, man, everybody's bailing,' he complained. 'I already got a medium with no takers. You want it?'

The guard happily took the pizza, and waved Bruce through the checkpoint.

As he headed down the hallway towards his old lab, Bruce suddenly started to feel nervous. This was the place where the experiment had ruined his life. But maybe that could change. Maybe now it could be where he put his life back on track.

The set-up had changed in the last five years. Bruce could see through the glass walls around the lab that, instead of physics equipment, it now held computer terminals, with large supercomputer arrays along the walls. A graduate student sat at a terminal, staring with bleary eyes.

Bruce opened the door. 'Those jerks in radiation called

this in and then split,' he remarked, pointing at the pizza. 'You want it?'

The grad student smiled. 'Whoever you are, you are my new personal hero.'

Bruce glanced around at all the computers. 'Hey,' he asked, 'you mind if I jump online for a second?'

'Totally, no problem,' the student replied, already opening the pizza box.

'Righteous,' Bruce said. He sat down at a terminal across from the student, and quickly accessed the university's main system, which requested a user name and a password.

Bruce typed in 'Dr Elizabeth Ross' for the user name, and then was momentarily stumped for Betty's password. He tried 'bettylovesbruce', which was rejected. Then he tried another old password of hers: 'Cells_Unite!'

Bingo! He quickly looked for records of his experiment, but searching under both 'USMD Research Protocol 456-72378' and 'Gamma Pulse' yielded no results.

He tried a few more searches before recognizing that no trace of the experiment existed at all in the system. The military must have had the records deleted completely! Bruce sagged in his chair, defeated.

With a sigh, Bruce realized that there was nothing left for him in that lab. It was time to go.

CHAPTER 11

'Gone, all of it,' Bruce told Stan that night in the pizza parlour's private back room. 'Like it never happened.'

'The whole building was closed for a year after the explosion,' Stan explained. 'Military guards . . .'

'There's nothing for me here,' Bruce said. 'I don't know why I came. I guess I'll go in the morning.'

'Where?' Stan asked.

'It's better if I don't tell you, Stan,' Bruce replied. 'You've helped me, though. You've got no idea how nice it is just to see a friendly face.'

The bell out in the pizza parlour dinged as customers entered, and Stan got up. 'Don't go anywhere yet,' he told Bruce as he headed towards the front room. 'It's about to rain. After these customers, I'll close up, and we'll have some real food.'

'Folks, I'm closing,' Stan said as he pushed through the swinging doors into the pizza parlour's main area. He was shocked to see Betty and Samson standing by the glass case by the register, but he tried not to show it.

'Come on, Stan, it's Friday night!' Betty said. 'Please!'

Samson put his arm round her. 'She worked through dinner again,' he added.

Stan hesitated, worried that Bruce might come out into the front room. But he couldn't resist the pleading look in Betty's eyes.

In the small guest room upstairs, Bruce was packing his belongings.

Stan cooked while Betty and Samson chatted. Never before had a pizza seemed to take so long to bake!

Bruce came back downstairs into the back room. 'Stan?' he called, pushing open the swinging parlour doors.

Betty looked up over Samson's shoulder to see who was there and gasped with shock. But then Samson shifted his position, blocking her view. When he moved again, Bruce had vanished.

Samson was saying something, but Betty couldn't hear a word. She just stared at the swinging doors. She then sprang past Samson into the back room. 'Bruce!' she yelled.

Bruce wasn't there, so Betty burst out through the back door into an alley. Thunder rumbled in the distance as the first raindrops began to fall. Betty quickly glanced left and right. 'Bruce!'

But there was no sign of him.

Little did Betty know, Bruce had flattened himself further behind a dumpster, holding his breath.

'Betty!' Samson called as he followed her. 'What's going on? Come inside.' The rain was already falling harder.

Betty strode back inside, shaking, heading straight for Stan who stood paralysed behind the parlour counter. 'Please don't lie to me,' Betty pleaded. 'That was Bruce, wasn't it?'

'Betty,' Stan began, agonized between protecting Bruce and lying to an old friend. 'I don't . . . know what to say.'

Betty took that as a yes. After quickly dropping Samson off at home, she drove into the dark thundershower, desperately searching for Bruce. She left the side streets and pulled on to a bigger road leading to the highway, where she spotted Bruce on the shoulder, hitch-hiking in the downpour.

He stuck out his thumb at an approaching car, and it stopped with a flash of red brake lights. The door burst open and Betty ran out, embracing Bruce tightly. 'Please don't go away,' Betty begged. 'I need to see you and talk to you. Come home with me.'

'I want to . . . so much,' Bruce replied. 'But it's not safe.'

'I don't care,' Betty said.

Bruce hid in the back of Betty's car until they were hidden inside the garage of the house she shared with Samson. When they entered the kitchen, they could hear Samson talking on the phone.

'Forgive me, but that contradicts everything you've told me,' Samson said. He turned around when he heard Betty and Bruce walk in. 'Hang on a moment . . . Tilda, it'll be fine. We'll pick this up in our session.' He smiled at Bruce as he hung up the phone. 'A patient,' he explained. He extended his hand and shook Bruce's warmly. 'Welcome,' Samson said. 'Now both of you get out of those wet clothes. I think we all need some hot food. You two talk while I cook.'

After they had changed, Betty drew the curtains, and she and Bruce settled down on couches. 'So you hid in Alaska?' Betty prompted.

Bruce nodded. 'It was peaceful up there on the northern plateau. For a long time that's all I wanted. When I heard that the rug dealer in town had got Internet access, I couldn't resist. That's how I got to Mr Blue.'

'Dr Samuel Sterns,' Betty said. 'He's been synthesizing a trimethadine inhibitor. Sterns has some kind of ethics cloud around him, but his work is so brilliant, it didn't stop him. So . . . you went to Brazil for the Callandras flower?'

'He's synthesizing trimethadine,' Bruce agreed, 'but I had to try to get it at the source. Unfortunately I couldn't get a thousandth of what I'd need. Now I go and find Sterns,

I suppose. It's a much longer shot without the data from the lab, though.'

Betty stood up and walked over to her bookshelf. She reached into a vase and pulled out a flash card on a lanyard, then handed it to Bruce. 'I got in there before they carted it all away,' Betty explained. 'I hoped it would be useful someday.'

Bruce stared at the data flash card in amazement. 'Sometimes hope just appears, so quickly,' he whispered. 'Does the general know you have this?'

'I don't think so,' Betty replied.

'Your father was in Brazil when they came for me,' Bruce told her. 'I saw him.'

Betty sat down next to Bruce. 'Oh, I'm so sorry,' she said. 'He's crazier than anybody knows. How did he find you?'

'I can't figure it out,' he said. 'Do you think it could have been Sterns?'

Betty shook her head. 'I hear he hates authority and doesn't think he should answer to anybody. That's why he got in trouble.' She squeezed Bruce's hand. 'I want to show you something.' Betty led Bruce into her office, where she pointed out a gorgeous, delicate orchid on the windowsill.

Bruce smiled. 'Oh . . .' he said breathlessly. 'You grew it. I knew you could.'

'It shouldn't survive here,' Betty replied. 'It took four

months just to cultivate the bacteria for the soil. I've almost lost it three or four times, but it held on somehow.'

Bruce slid his finger along the orchid's exotic stem. 'I sent you those seeds to let you know I was –'

'I know,' Betty replied. 'I –'

'Ah, my rival for her affection,' Samson broke in. He peered down at the orchid. 'Between work and this little guy, I have to fight for a position.'

After dinner they all headed upstairs to sleep. Bruce shook Samson's hand in the hallway, and Betty led Bruce to a spare room. 'Do you need anything?' she asked.

'No,' he answered. 'I should go early tomorrow. If I can borrow cash from you, I'll take the bus.'

'Of course,' Betty said quickly. 'I'll drive you out to the station.' Bruce looked so tired and lonely that it was hard for her to leave him, but she forced herself to say good night.

CHAPTER 12

When Bruce woke up in the morning, heavy thunder was rumbling in the distance. Another big storm was on the way.

Bruce got dressed, cinching the belt and fastening his too-big jeans. He stepped into the hallway where he could hear Betty and Samson talking softly in the kitchen downstairs. As he padded down the steps, he couldn't help overhearing.

'Then I'm going to walk him there,' Betty was saying.

'We'll call a cab for him,' Samson replied.

'No,' Betty argued. 'I'm going with –'

She stopped her sentence and waved briefly to Bruce when he entered the kitchen. 'The car battery seems to be dead,' she told him. 'I must have left the lights on. The station's only a mile away, though . . . You okay to walk it?'

Walking left him open to being discovered, but what other choice did he have? He nodded. 'Thank you,' he said. 'For everything.'

'Good luck,' Samson said.

Bruce faced Betty. He could tell that Samson didn't want her coming with him. He didn't want to cause any more trouble than he already had. 'We shouldn't leave here together,' he warned.

Betty picked up her purse. 'Samson can show you to the back door,' she said. 'Remember our bench . . . by the library? I'll meet you there.'

The campus was quiet when Betty arrived at the Culver library. She walked nervously on the familiar path towards the bench. Bruce's caution made her feel edgy, too. When she reached the bench, she peered around, looking for him.

Bruce emerged from behind a tree and joined her. They both faced each other, but Bruce's gaze kept flickering around. He was on high alert.

'Is everything okay?' Betty asked.

Bruce nodded. 'Ready?' he asked.

Betty agreed, and they headed across campus in the direction of the bus station. Most of the students were still asleep. As they walked Betty studied Bruce, taking in his old shirt tucked into too-big jeans, his ill-fitting cap. She stopped him, pulled off his cap and adjusted its strap – an old habit of hers.

Bruce stared at her, chewing on his lip as she replaced his cap.

'What is it?' Betty asked.

'Seeing Culver again, I keep trying to remember . . .' Bruce began. 'What were we trying to accomplish that was worth all this trouble?'

Betty thought about the question. 'I think we were trying to understand something,' she said finally. 'Advance things a little. Make a difference.'

'I think that's what we told ourselves, because it sounded noble,' said Bruce. 'At least the general was honest about what he wanted out of it. I don't think we were as honest. We were trying to show how smart we were, and we broke the rules.'

Betty sighed. 'No,' she said. 'You're being too hard on yourself. We did talk about it, and we were all comfortable. The worst you can say is that you rushed it. But you didn't ask anyone else to take the risk for you.'

'It wasn't me who got hurt,' Bruce replied.

Betty bit her lip. 'None of us thought something like that was possible,' she said. 'How could we have –?'

'Why not?' Bruce broke in. 'Nature takes a long time to build us like we are. Then we come in with our big brains and think we can improve it overnight. Why are we so surprised when it blows up in our faces?'

Thunder rumbled again; the storm was getting closer. The clouds on the far edge of the university darkened with the approaching rain.

'I have to stop my mind from replaying the . . . explosion,'

Betty said. 'It's like a bad dream . . . It still doesn't seem possible it was real. But it *was* real, wasn't it?'

Before he could answer, Bruce caught a glimpse of a quick movement across the central quad. His eyes darted towards the spot, just beyond the far edge of a building where he'd seen something duck back. He spotted a sniper, adjusting for position.

He grabbed Betty's shoulders. 'Oh, no.' He groaned. 'They're here.'

'What – who –?' Betty sputtered.

'Go home,' Bruce ordered. 'Get as far away from me as you can! Go!'

He broke away from her and bolted across the lawn.

CHAPTER 13

All along the lawn soldiers exploded out from behind columns and trees, charging after Bruce.

Bruce sped into a sprint, weaving, desperate to outdistance the soldiers.

Hearing engines behind her, Betty spun around and gasped at the two Humvees roaring down the quad's perimeter. They smashed parked cars, splitting up and racing on either side of her – one bumping up on to the grass, the other zooming down the road. One had a .50-caliber Browning machine gun on its roof.

Betty chased after them.

Bruce dashed off, taking a hard turn down a columned walkway. The buildings opened up beyond a courtyard, into a field, and he bolted towards that exit. Past the field, Bruce knew, was a large patch of forest.

On the monitors in their black van, General Ross and Major Sparr watched Banner run. 'No!' Ross shouted, furious that his trap had been sprung too soon.

Bruce whipped through a small grove of trees and reached the field, accelerating across the open ground. Along the edges of the field were the outer buildings of the campus – like the back of the library facility, which was connected to a performing-arts centre by a glassed-in overpass. Ahead of Bruce was a huge steel Modern art sculpture.

Bruce veered slightly when Humvees appeared on the far edge of the performing-arts centre. From his new angle he could see the two vehicles motoring towards him from behind. He focused on the line of forest across the field – his only hope of escape.

'Target on the run,' Sparr announced over the radio. 'Sniper Two has the shot. Straight at your twelve, Blonsky.'

At the exact spot where Banner was heading, Blonsky was hiding in the underbrush, ready with a .308 sniper rifle.

Blonsky peered through his sniper scope, aiming at Banner who was cresting a rise in the field. 'Target sighted,' Blonsky informed the officers.

Scanning the edge of the woods, Bruce spotted a glare from the sniper. He stopped dead in his tracks.

Blonsky cursed as the target stopped short. Banner seemed to stare right into the crosshairs of his scope, and then he abruptly broke left and Blonsky missed the shot.

Another bullet whizzed by Bruce, forcing him to lurch in the other direction, dashing past the large modern sculpture.

Blonsky sighed, then raised his microphone to his mouth. 'We've been seen. He's heading for those outer buildings.'

Blonsky immediately pulled ahead, running at an impossibly fast pace. He carried his heavy rifle in one hand, like it weighed nothing.

Bruce tore round the corner of the arts centre and hurtled across a stone terrace. He sped towards the back doors of the library, burst inside, and raced down a narrow aisle between tall bookshelves.

A dozen soldiers followed him in while others surrounded the building.

When Betty neared the library, she stopped, taking in the swarm of soldiers around the building, with more pouring out of mobile transports and taking positions around the metal sculpture. Another team was sprinting from the forest. Far to the right were Humvees holding strange, bulky equipment. She spotted a black command van slowing near a transport and hustled towards it.

Inside the library, Bruce jumped up a narrow staircase and raced down another aisle, dropping to his knees between two shelves. He yanked the data flash card out of his pocket and removed its lanyard. Soldiers' footsteps clattered nearby, climbing the stairs towards him.

Bruce opened his mouth and shoved the data card

down his throat. He forced himself to swallow it, coughing and gagging. There was no way he was going to lose the data again. No way. As soon as it was down, Bruce peeked out from behind the shelf, just as a soldier looked his way. The soldier yelled, and Bruce darted down the aisle.

Betty caught up to the black van. She banged on the tinted window. 'I know it's you!' she shouted. 'General, come out of there!'

The van door opened, and her father stepped out. General Ross faced her impatiently, glancing over at the buildings. Two rangers guarded him from behind with their rifles.

'Please don't do this,' Betty begged. 'He needs help!'

'You can't see this clearly,' Ross snapped at her. 'Now get inside.' He reached out to grab her arm, but she pulled away.

Bruce burst through the double doors of the overpass and into the glass-enclosed tube, running towards the performing-arts centre.

'There he is!' one of Ross's rangers shouted.

Everybody on the field watched Banner bolting through the overpass. Above the buildings, ominous thunderclouds gathered, turning the sky a deep grey.

When commandos appeared on the side of the performing-arts building, Bruce stopped short and spun around to run back to the library. But soldiers were waiting for him there, too. He stood in the middle of the overpass, trapped, his chest heaving, as he pondered his next move.

'Do not engage!' Ross barked over the radio. He motioned to Sparr. 'Ready the special unit in the north end of the field,' he ordered her. 'If he changes, he'll try to make for the forest, and that's where we'll hit him with our surprise.'

'The buildings will take a direct hit,' Sparr warned. 'If there's anyone in them –'

'Do it!' Ross barked.

Sparr flicked on her radio transmitter. 'DISCO's online,' she announced. 'Set up overlapping fields and seal off the north end.'

Whoomp. As the strange machines on the Humvees cycled on, a deep hum echoed across the field, and an eerie rumble vibrated across the ground.

Ross tightened his hands to fists. 'Put canisters in that overpass,' he ordered. 'One on either side.'

Soldiers cornering Bruce quickly backed out, bolting the doors. Bruce stared at them in momentary confusion, but then he saw two missiles heading for the walkway. He ducked as small canisters broke through the glass. They clanked on the ceiling, clattered on to the floor, and then issued out clouds of thick smoke.

Bruce ripped off his shirt, then took a deep gasp of air and balled up the shirt over his mouth and nose.

'Bruce!' Betty screamed as she saw the tube fill with

smoke. She broke away from her father and dashed towards the overpass.

'Get her back here!' Ross shouted, and his rangers scrambled after her.

Bruce's pulse throbbed and he flailed around as he tried to stay in pockets of clean air. He pushed up against the glass, and his eyes widened when he saw a soldier reach Betty and grab her arm. She elbowed him and broke free. Bruce cried out as the other ranger tackled her to the ground.

Bruce dropped his shirt and pressed himself flat against the wall. Burning rage sizzled through his body, and his eyes flashed green. His chest heaved and contorted, his torso twisting as he tumbled back into the smoke.

Betty screamed as the smoke lit up with a flare of brilliant green.

In the van, all the radiation monitors spiked.

'The Geiger counter's lighting up!' Sparr yelled.

Ross didn't take his eyes off the smoke-filled overpass.

His real target was about to arrive.

CHAPTER 14

'Keep cameras on him!' Ross shouted.

Bruce contorted in agony inside the smoky tube. Green energy surged downward from the base of his skull, flowing down his face and neck, shimmering in his arms.

Betty struggled to her knees, staring up at the overpass. An arm and hand slapped on to the glass, clawing at it desperately. The hand glowed green, and the whole arm swelled, plumping with thick muscle before sliding back into the smoke. Bruce howled in anguish as he changed. His foot, green and throbbing, exploded out of his brown leather boot.

Everyone watched the tube as the smoke churned. A huge shadow shifted in the smoke, rising with his back to them. The enormous creature turned and spread wide his massive arms. He smashed his fists into the glass, and the windows along the whole tube shattered. Smoke poured out, and the soldiers could see the giant, green creature, packed from head to toe with rounded bricks of solid muscle. He snarled and leaped to the ground, smoke trailing behind him. When he landed, with one knee bent, the ground trembled from the impact.

The Hulk slowly rose to his full, gargantuan height, and all the soldiers on the field took a step backwards.

Sparr's jaw dropped. 'This was not in the recruitment video,' she said with a gasp.

With three powerful strides, The Hulk cleared the courtyard, pounding towards the open field. He spotted Betty on the ground, with General Ross beyond her, and he roared with rage, shaking his boulder-size fists in the air.

'We're going to Bravo,' Ross instructed. 'Move him towards the cannons. Keep your cool. Alpha Team, hit him with everything you've got.'

A barrage of machine-gun fire pounded into the beast's right flank. Six soldiers with assault rifles stood near the metal sculpture, shooting along with another commando using a machine gun on a tripod.

The creature threw up an arm to ward off the stinging rounds. Instead of being driven left, the creature turned and charged towards the statue. He raised his hand like a shield, heavy rounds pounding into his palm and raking down his legs. But he didn't stop storming ahead. The soldiers scattered as he got closer.

'Get Betty out of there!' Sparr commanded the rangers. They grabbed her and hustled her away.

Ross swore softly, watching as the giant moved in the wrong direction. 'Get that fifty on him!' he instructed. 'Move!'

The Humvee with the .50-caliber gun on its roof accelerated towards the sculpture. As it pulled up alongside the giant, the gunner opened fire.

The creature kept running, pelted by bullets. Then suddenly he vanished. The gunner in the Humvee peered around, bewildered by The Hulk's disappearance.

The creature had leaped straight up. He landed with an earthshaking thump in front of the Humvee and walloped his fists down into the vehicle's engine block. The Humvee jacked up, like a skateboard. The Hulk raised his fists high and smashed the front of the vehicle again, crushing its hood into the ground.

He grabbed the Humvee and heaved it into the air, shook the soldiers loose, and then began to slam the Humvee repeatedly into the twenty-foot steel sculpture. The Humvee disintegrated in an explosion of metal and petrol. Thunder cracked across the sky as the beast let out a mighty bellow.

'Where is my gunship?' Ross barked at Sparr.

Sparr bent over her radio. 'Base,' she ordered, 'get that bird in the air ASAP!'

'All right, keep your cool!' Ross told his troops. 'If you can't push him, get him to chase you. Either way, move him towards those cannons!' he barked.

Soldiers up in the overpass fired at The Hulk with assault rifles. Blonsky stepped forward, firing as he approached. Blonsky blasted the creature with his sniper rifle, but the rounds slammed uselessly into his target.

Peppered by bullets ricocheting off his enormous back, the giant heaved his shoulder against one of the sculpture's metal plates and tore off a big, flat chunk of the artwork. He held its centre bolt like the handle of a huge shield. Then the creature pulled on a second giant plate. It tore free with rivets popping and a screech of metal.

'This is a joke,' Blonsky snapped. 'Cover me!' He dropped his rifle and snatched a revolving grenade launcher from the soldier beside him who was frozen in fear. Blonsky charged at the monster.

The creature held up both metal plates, shaking them angrily in the air. One of the plates had a jagged torn edge, like a circular saw's blade. He lowered the metal shields when something hard and heavy struck the back of his head, and he roared in surprise when it exploded. Then another one hit him and detonated, stinging his legs. The giant turned and saw a man standing behind him, repeatedly firing grenades.

'Remember me?' Blonsky asked.

The creature howled, and lurched after Blonsky, wielding the metal plates like colossal slicing scythes.

Blonsky dodged the big blades, leaping and ducking

with his enhanced strength and speed as he ran, all the while turning back and firing his grenades at close range.

'He's doing it!' Ross cheered in the van. 'DISCO's on deck,' he announced.

Blonsky, with his superspeed, pulled away from The Hulk as it chased him. Ahead of him were the two Humvees, fifty yards apart. On each was a massive disc, like a giant stereo speaker, pointing at an angle towards campus.

With another burst of speed, Blonsky dashed into the speakers' range, with the creature hot on his tail. The soldiers operating the speakers hesitated, unsure if they should fire with Blonsky in the way.

'Hit him!' Blonsky howled. 'Now!'

The operators fired the sonic cannons, unleashing two murderous cones of low-frequency sound. Huge circular waves expanded as they warped the air.

Before he could be caught in the sonic waves, Blonsky dived twenty feet into the safety zone. He rolled when he hit the ground and popped back up to watch the fireworks.

The first blast of sound hit the beast squarely on his left side, knocking him down on his right knee. Then the second wave hit him, pounding him from the right side in a crushing crossfire. The creature's hands flew up to his ears, trying to block his overamplified senses from the insanely painful noise.

The sonic waves expanded past The Hulk, decimating

everything in their path. Trees vibrated and split down the middle. The windows in the buildings shattered. The soldiers in the overpass scrambled as the glass structure shuddered into fragments.

The Hulk bellowed with unbelievable pain. He crouched down, his green skin rippling under the sonic assault. Dark green blood trickled from his ears as his brain started to scramble.

He lurched forward on to one fist, trying weakly to hold himself up.

'Stop it!' Betty shrieked from the van. 'You're killing him!'

CHAPTER 15

Betty broke free from the soldier's clutches and sprinted across the field. The rangers bolted after her. They caught Betty, holding her fast.

She strained against their grip. 'Bruce!' she screeched.

A confused look crossed the giant's face at the sound of that name. He shuddered, and a green pulse flared, surging out from his skull. New strength flooded into his body, and his colossal muscles swelled with greater power.

Slowly the creature heaved himself up, using the steel plates as supports. When he reached his feet, the creature roared. Then he lifted the plates up from the ground, spread his arms wide, and smashed the shields together, like giant cymbals. The crash was intensely loud, and its vibrations cleared the sonic waves for a second. In that moment of freedom, the creature hurled one plate at the cannon on the left, like a vast throwing star. The spinning steel panel sliced it in half.

The sound waves from the right cannon refocused, but the creature held his other shield up. The deadly waves bounced off the metal plate, surging around it. The beast pushed the plate towards the remaining cannon, advancing into the powerful sonic wave.

The soldiers fired at The Hulk, stinging his legs, but he kept heaving forward. When he got close, he crouched and leaped up out of the cone of sound.

The Hulk landed with his shield flat, smashing directly on to the cannon. The whole rear of the Humvee crushed into a neat square. Silence descended across the battlefield as the giant stepped off the flattened Humvee, holding his shield in his left hand.

Ross slammed his fist on the dashboard, furious.

The radio crackled. 'Two minutes out, Major,' the pilot reported to Sparr.

Ross took a deep breath. 'All positions, engage him,' he ordered. 'Keep him busy. Prepare to fall back on my order.'

None of the soldiers moved. Nobody dared to engage that creature – except Blonsky. He found an assault rifle and rushed at The Hulk. When he got close, he unloaded a full clip into the beast's back.

The creature slowly turned around to face him, but he stayed strangely still, staring down at the small soldier.

The radio in the van squawked again. 'Closing in,' the pilot reported. 'What's the target?'

Sparr checked the monitor. 'From my position, three

hundred yards,' she replied. 'It's ten feet tall and green.'

'Come again?' the pilot asked.

'You heard right,' Ross snapped. 'Put everything you've got on him. Ground teams, pull back.'

Blonsky stepped sideways, and the creature continued to stare at him. 'Come on, Banner,' the soldier yelled. 'That all you got?'

'Blonsky, fall back now!' Ross ordered over the radio.

The creature's eyes narrowed with hatred as it glared at Blonsky. He twitched his giant shield as though he might swing it.

'Come on,' Blonsky taunted. 'Let's see what else you've got –'

Smash! The Hulk snapped out his foot and whacked into Blonsky, instantly breaking every bone in his body. The crushed commando hurtled fifty yards backward and skidded across the grass, like a broken doll.

'Oh, no!' Sparr gasped.

Ross's jaw clenched in dismay.

Thunder cracked in the dark sky, and it started to rain as The Hulk stomped towards Betty.

'Fall back and find cover!' Ross ordered his troops.

Betty stepped closer to The Hulk just as an Apache gunship helicopter buzzed over the line of trees, hovering into position.

Inside the gunship, the targeting computer locked its

crosshairs on to the giant . . . but did not see Betty on the other side. She raised her hand up to touch The Hulk's giant, green arm. 'Bruce?' she whispered.

The creature grumbled as a spark of dim recognition flashed in his eyes.

Ross and Sparr hustled away for cover from the van, with the rest of the troops. Sparr glanced back to check the progress of the rangers who had been holding Betty. They were hurrying across a road without her.

Sparr spotted Betty standing with The Hulk, but Ross didn't seem to notice where his daughter was. 'Fire!' he ordered the Apache.

'Hold on to your hats,' the pilot replied.

Sparr waved her arms frantically. 'Hold fire!' she screamed.

But it was too late. The Apache's two rotating cannons unloaded, tearing up the earth around Betty and The Hulk.

Betty instinctively pressed her body against the creature for shelter.

Powerful rounds pounded into the giant's back, slicing up the flesh of his legs, tearing the skin on his shoulder blades. Keeping Betty behind him, he wheeled around to face the onslaught.

The battle helicopter accelerated towards him in order to concentrate its attack. It zipped closer, low to the ground. The Hulk twisted his body, like a discus thrower, and he hurled his giant plate through the air. It ripped through the tower of the gunship's propeller, cleanly cleaving off the main rotor.

The pilot leaped out as the Apache went down nose first. The gunship ploughed into the ground. The Hulk grabbed Betty, wrapping himself around her for protection as he turned his back to the tumbling aircraft. The helicopter exploded as it rolled, engulfing the giant in flames.

The concussion of the blast knocked everyone who was watching the event to the ground. Ross raised his head, staring at the inferno. There was no way his daughter could have survived the blast.

But then The Hulk stepped out of the flames, his face contorted with pain. He was cradling Betty in his powerful arms. Lightning split the sky as the rain poured down. The Hulk stood snarling at Ross, still sheltering Betty against his massive chest.

A crack of jarring thunder boomed, and The Hulk began to run. He lurched across the field, past the soldiers and wreckage, past Blonsky's crumpled body. His strides lengthening with each step.

He disappeared into the darkness of the forest.

CHAPTER 16

The Hulk crashed deep into the stormy forest, pushing his way through the trees for hours until he reached the base of the Smoky Mountains. He climbed the foothills, and then spotted a cave opening in the jagged rocks.

He extended his arms into the cave, gently laying Betty down in a dry spot.

As soon as he let go, Betty started awake. She gasped; confused when she saw the monstrous face. Betty let out a small scream and slapped his giant cheek.

The creature growled, surprised by the slap.

'Oh, no,' Betty moaned, realizing who he was. 'I'm sorry.'

The Hulk stood by the entrance of the cave; he couldn't fit inside fully.

Betty wrapped her arms around herself in the cold cave. She took her handbag strap off her shoulder and removed her wet raincoat, shaking it out and then draping it over herself, like a blanket. She looked up at The Hulk.

He pulled away, groaning. In his vision, Betty looked

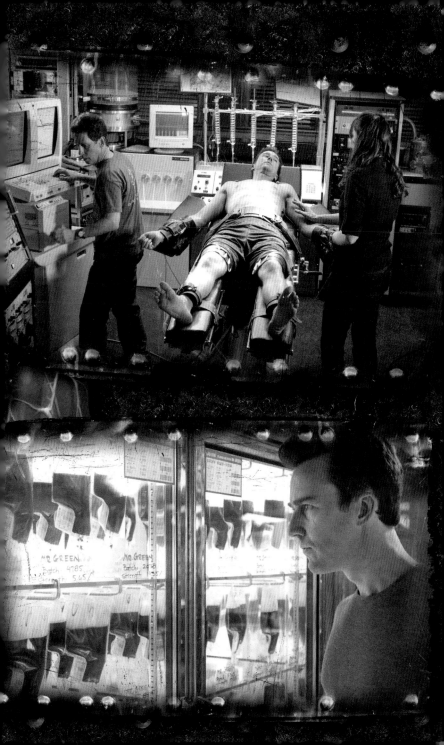

warped and distorted, bizarrely fractured in two. The sound of the rain sizzled, like acid.

'Bruce, can you understand me?' Betty asked.

Her voice soothed him, and he settled down for a second – until a bright flash of lightning exploded in the sky.

The creature roared; the blast of light terrified and enraged him. He whipped around, searching for the source of the attack. When lightning flickered again, he grabbed a boulder and hurled it up at the sky.

'It's okay!' Betty called to him. 'We're okay.' She stepped out of the cave into the rain, then touched the creature gently on his arm.

He turned abruptly, growling at her, but Betty wasn't afraid. She put her hand on one of his fingers and peered at his arm. She gasped in amazement when she saw that the gashes in his arm were knitting up rapidly.

'Come here,' she said soothingly, inviting him to sit beside her under the cave's overhanging ledge. 'Come on.' She gave him a tug, and he sat down beside her, out of the rain.

Ross strode into the army hospital and caught up with a doctor. 'Will Blonsky walk again?' he demanded to know.

The doctor stopped short. 'Most of his bones look like crushed gravel right now,' he replied. 'If he lives, he'll be lucky if he can lift a straw to eat his liquid meals.'

Ross winced as he followed the doctor into Blonsky's intensive care room. The soldier was completely bandaged, with every machine imaginable hooked up to him.

The doctor peered down at a clipboard. 'I will say this, though,' he told Ross, 'he's got a heart like a racehorse.'

In the morning Betty woke up to find Bruce sleeping beside her.

She sat up quietly and stared at him. He looked exhausted and weak, but his skin was smooth – all his wounds had healed completely.

When he woke, Bruce felt sick and miserable, but they made their way out of the mountains to a small town with a motel. Betty rented a room while Bruce hid behind an ice machine, wearing her raincoat and his shredded trousers.

Betty helped him into the room, then left to buy supplies while he showered.

When she came back with shopping bags, Betty heard Bruce vomiting in the bathroom. She put down her purchases on the bed and waited, concerned.

Bruce finally emerged from the bathroom with wet hair, not looking as bad as Betty feared.

'You okay?' she asked.

'Yeah, I feel better, actually,' he replied. He held up the flash card. 'Just getting this back.'

'Oh, the data!' Betty exclaimed. Then she looked concerned again. 'You *ate* it?'

'Yeah,' Bruce said sheepishly. 'Under the circumstances I had to improvise.'

'Wow,' Betty said. She pointed towards the bed. 'They didn't have much selection, but I got you a few options. First things first . . .'

She pulled a small box out of a bag and tossed it to him.

Bruce glanced down at a new pulse monitor. 'You're kidding me.'

'Got to love superstores,' Betty chirped. 'Okay, now, it's no Armani, but . . .' She began to pull clothes out of the bags, holding them up so he could see the sizes. Most were too small, and he gave those the thumbs-down. Then she handed him a pair of stretchy purple trousers.

He held them up to his waist. 'I'm an irradiated freak,' he said, tossing them back to her, 'but that doesn't mean I've lost my sense of style.'

Betty laughed. 'They were the stretchiest ones they had!'

'I'll take my chances,' he said, sitting down on the bed beside her.

Betty reached up and gently touched a scar under his eye. 'All the other ones are gone,' she said softly.

'That one's mine,' Bruce said. 'His heal. Mine don't.'

'Yes, they do,' Betty replied. 'They leave a mark, but

they stop hurting.' She brushed her fringe away from her forehead, revealing the scar she'd got in the explosion that had turned him into The Hulk.

Bruce looked away. That scar was a symbol of everything he feared he was becoming.

'No, look at me,' Betty insisted. 'That pain didn't last. Not knowing was so much worse. It took me two years to keep myself from looking for you in crowds. I stopped looking, but I never stopped hoping.'

Bruce let out a deep breath. He turned around, and slowly lowered his face to her forehead and gently kissed her scar.

CHAPTER 17

Ross paced across his office as he watched the news reports on TV. He grimaced as they showed footage of the final explosion.

The coverage switched to a reporter in a newsroom. 'Rumours continue to swirl about a clash between the US military and an unknown adversary at Culver University earlier today,' the reporter announced. 'We know that authorities have renewed the long-cold hunt for fugitive government scientist Robert Bruce Banner.' A picture of Banner appeared over the reporter's shoulder, and Ross glared at it.

The TV now showed a blonde reporter standing with two students on campus. 'Very few outside the military got a first-hand look at who – or what – the soldiers were fighting,' she said. 'Sophomores Jack McGhee and Jim Wilson were coming home from a hike and witnessed some of the battle. McGhee captured this on his mobile phone.' The screen flashed an extremely grainy image of the creature.

The reporter held up her microphone to the nearest

student, Jack McGhee. 'Can you describe what you saw?' she asked.

'Dude, it was huge and green!' McGhee exclaimed.

'Dude, it was so big,' Wilson agreed. 'It was like this huge . . . hulk.'

The reporter faced the camera again. 'Further search for the mysterious 'hulk' was delayed by powerful thunderstorms in Smoky Mountain National Park.'

Ross wheeled around when Sparr entered his office.

'It's Blonsky,' said Sparr.

Ross and Sparr hustled towards the hospital ward. As they pushed through the ICU doors, he asked, 'Has anybody found out if he has family?'

Sparr held open the door for him. 'You can ask him yourself,' she replied.

A group of doctors and nurses backed away from Blonsky's bed as Ross entered, and Ross could see Blonsky sitting up, laughing. He was completely healed. The super-soldier serum had made him stronger than ever.

Blonsky grinned when he saw Ross. 'Sir,' he said.

Ross shook his hand, astounded at the recovery. 'Good to see you alive, soldier. How do you feel?'

Blonsky's grin widened. 'Ready for round three,' he replied.

Betty emptied out the contents of her handbag on to the motel bedspread. She had a phone, a credit and bank card, her driver's licence, seventy dollars in cash, some make-up, her university ID and a digital camera.

Betty shrugged. 'I thought if you asked me to go, I ought to be ready.'

Bruce smiled, touched that she was prepared to join him. He collected everything from the bedspread, except the money and the camera, and put them back into her bag. 'We can't use any of it but the cash,' he said. 'Don't even turn the phone on – they can track it.'

'How about my lipstick?' Betty joked. 'Can they track that?'

With a laugh, Bruce said, 'No, you can keep that.'

Betty looked down at the money in his hand. 'We can't get where we're going on seventy bucks, can we?'

'Not quickly enough,' Bruce replied.

'We can pawn this,' Betty said. She removed a chain from her neck, pulling up a lovely gold pendant.

'No,' Bruce said firmly. 'It's the only thing of your mother's that you have.'

'We'll get it back,' Betty promised.

Ross stood in the Pentagon planning room, looking over the team he had assembled as Sparr wrapped up the briefing on the Banner situation. They all stared up at Bruce's and Betty's photos on the projection screen.

'Federal is already monitoring phone, plastic, and Dr Ross's Web accounts, and local police are on alert,' Sparr continued. 'They'll pop up somewhere.'

Ross cleared his throat. 'They won't pop up,' he contradicted. 'Banner made it five years and got across borders without making a mistake. He won't use a credit card now. He's not trying to escape this time – he's looking for help.' The general raised a hand and closed it into a fist. '*That's* how we're going to get him. There are only a few hundred people in the world who have what he needs. Figure out who they are – he's going to one of them.'

Betty counted out cash to the young guy working at the counter at a petrol station. While the clerk was distracted, Bruce stepped into the attached garage and spotted a greasy-looking computer terminal on a desk. He plugged the data card into the computer.

He typed a quick e-mail to Dr Sterns that read, 'What you requested is attached. Maybe it's time to meet. Green.' Then he uploaded the data from the card and sent it off.

Betty came out of the shop as he exited the garage. She held up a set of keys and smiled, pointing at a battered pick-up truck. Betty got in the driver's side, and Bruce took shotgun. As Bruce removed the FOR SALE sign from the window, Betty said, 'Hey . . .'

Bruce faced her, then grimaced when he saw her holding up the camera.

'It's been worse than this before, right?' Betty asked.

'Yes,' Bruce replied. 'Much worse.'

'And you're not just running now,' Betty continued. 'We're on the way to something better. So smile.'

Bruce raised his lips in a sad, uncertain smile, and she snapped the picture.

They were still on the highway as night fell. Betty drove, and Bruce leaned his head against the passenger-side window, staring moodily out into the dark.

'Penny for your thoughts,' Betty said.

Bruce sat up straight. 'How long have you known Samson?'

'About a year and a half,' Betty answered. 'Why?'

'Do you . . . trust him?' Bruce asked.

'Yes, I do,' she replied, her voice growing sharp. 'Bruce, you know that I –'

'You don't have to explain anything to me,' Bruce broke in. 'He seems like a good man, and he treats you well. That makes me happy.'

'He does,' Betty said carefully. 'But . . . I never trusted

him with this.' She adjusted her hands on the steering wheel. 'I didn't test his faith in me by asking him to believe something impossible.'

'Who could?' Bruce said. 'Sometimes I even convince myself it's not real.'

Betty took a deep breath. 'Do you remember anything . . . when it happens?'

'Just fragments.'

'But then it's still you . . . inside him,' Betty said.

'It's not me,' Bruce responded curtly.

Betty let that sit before replying. 'Okay, but . . .' she began, 'in the cave, I felt that you knew . . . that *he* knew me. Maybe your mind is in there, but just overcharged. You can't process what's happening.'

'I want to get rid of him,' Bruce said sullenly. 'He hurts people. He almost killed you. I didn't do those things!'

'Of course not,' Betty said.

Bruce turned away from her, staring out of the window into the darkness.

All he could see was his own reflection.

CHAPTER 18

In a secret medical lab Blonsky sat back on a hospital bed. Two nearby technicians prepared syringes of super-soldier serum, while another one hooked Blonsky up to monitors.

Ross stepped up to the edge of the bed. 'You ready?' he asked.

Blonsky smiled. 'Let's even the game a little,' he replied.

Bruce woke up in the truck sometime in the afternoon. They were inching down the highway in heavy traffic, and he couldn't tell how long he'd been asleep. On the radio, an announcer softly recited the news.

'I thought I should let you rest,' Betty said.

'Where are we?' Bruce asked, rubbing his eyes.

'Stuck in traffic,' Betty replied. 'But we're getting close.'

Bruce peered out the front windshield at the traffic jam. The reporter on the radio mentioned traffic delays due to a heightened security alert, and Bruce opened his door and looked out. Far ahead, he could see the gates of a tollbooth at the entrance to the Holland Tunnel. Uniformed officers stood by the gates, staring at faces in the cars slowly passing the checkpoint.

'Let's go,' Bruce decided.

Betty glanced at him in alarm. 'Go where?'

'We've got to get out,' Bruce said. 'Let's go.'

Both of them exited the truck, abandoning it on the road. Picking their way through the slow lines of honking cars, they headed for the shoulder and hiked down a gravelly slope.

They made their way through an industrial area of Jersey City to the edge of the Hudson River. There Bruce spotted a dock in the distance. They approached one of the fishermen, a tall guy with a mop of grey hair who was leaning against a railing with a fishing pole. Betty chatted with him, offering him some money. The fisherman nodded.

A few minutes later they took a seat in a small outboard motorboat. The fisherman throttled the engine, and Bruce and Betty faced forward as they puttered out on to the river. New York City shimmered in the sunlight across the water.

They docked near Battery Park, thanked the fisherman, and walked up on to the streets of the city. Betty and Bruce stopped by a map kiosk to figure out the best route to their destination.

'It's a long way uptown,' Betty pointed out. 'The subway's the quickest way to get there.'

Bruce chuckled. 'Me in a crowded metal tube

underground with hundreds of other people in the most aggressive city in the world?'

'Bad idea,' said Betty. 'Let's get a cab.'

The cab driver who picked them up was easily the most reckless driver in a city full of reckless drivers.

Betty gasped as the taxi slashed wildly across two lanes on Sixth Avenue. The driver slammed on the brakes randomly, honked his horn every few seconds, nearly killed a bike messenger, and sped through yellow lights instead of slowing down for them. The radio blared crazy music while the driver jabbered on his mobile phone. Bruce and Betty slammed around in the back seat.

Bruce's new pulse monitor beeped as his heart rate climbed past ninety-seven beats per minute . . . up to ninety-eight . . . then ninety-nine . . .

He put his head back and closed his eyes, breathing deeply.

The cab screeched to a halt near Columbus Circle, in midtown Manhattan, bumping into the kerb by an entrance to Central Park. Betty and Bruce pushed the door open and piled out. They weren't close to their destination, but they couldn't stand that insane ride any longer!

Betty chucked a few dollars through the passenger-side window. 'That was the worst ride I've ever had!' she scolded.

The driver just made a kissing noise and screeched away.

Betty kicked the rear bumper as it passed her. 'Jerk!'

she yelled, letting out all of her pent-up frustration.

'You know,' Bruce suggested softly, 'I can show you some techniques to help you manage that rage a little better.'

'Zip it,' Betty snapped. 'We're walking.'

In her small office, Sparr peered down at a stack of files, sifting the information for any lead on where Banner might be heading. She looked up when an intelligence officer entered with another stack of manila folders.

'These are the ones they say could fit the profile,' the officer said as he dumped the files on her desk.

Sparr perked up – that had potential!

'Uh . . . just in Scandinavia alone,' the officer continued, and Sparr's face fell. She sighed and nodded as the officer left.

Sparr rubbed her temples, staring at her computer screen. She shrugged, struck by an impulsive idea. She navigated to Google on her browser and searched for 'Mr Blue cellular biology'.

She peered at the links that popped up. The first one she clicked brought her to a YouTube video.

In the video, a scientist named Samuel Sterns was holding a press conference to demonstrate a scientific breakthrough. 'Full cell saturation, a method of moving compounds into every cell in the body, will revolutionize medical therapies . . .' the scientist intoned.

Sparr was about to click back to Google when the scientist inserted a vial of blue dye into a machine that was hooked up to a graduate student's arm.

The audience laughed and applauded as the student slowly turned blue.

'What's his name?' a student in the audience asked.

'Who, Mr Blue here?' Dr Sterns joked.

Sparr bolted forward, her eyes wide. She closed the YouTube window and got back to Google. She quickly searched for 'Samuel Sterns cellular biology'.

A link came up for Empire State University. Sparr clicked to it and found a photo of Professor Samuel Sterns, the same man as in the video. The Mr Blue thing couldn't be a coincidence.

She ran down the hall into General Ross's office, bursting with the news. 'They're going to New York!' she declared.

CHAPTER 19

Outside Empire State University's science building, Professor Sterns walked down the front steps, shuffling a stack of papers in his hands.

Betty hurried over to him. 'Excuse me, Dr Sterns?' she said. 'Sorry to bother you. I'm Elizabeth Ross.'

Dr Sterns stared at her in surprise. 'Dr Ross, my goodness,' he replied with a gasp. 'I devoured your paper on synthesizing myostatin! To what do I owe the pleasure?'

Betty waved to Bruce, who strode up the stairs to join them. 'There's someone who would like to meet you,' Betty said.

Bruce stuck out his hand for the professor to shake. 'It's Mr Blue, isn't it?'

Dr Sterns's mouth dropped open. 'Mr Green!'

Up in Dr Sterns's office, Bruce and Betty stepped through a mad scientist's clutter of books, papers, chemical models and scientific equipment. There was nowhere for guests to sit, so they stood in front of the professor's messy desk.

Dr Sterns plopped down in his desk chair, chattering

away happily. 'That you survived a gamma event like that and then stand here and discuss this is just amazing,' he told Bruce. 'It has something to do with Dr Ross's myostatin protecting the cells, of course, but it's beyond my reckoning . . . We could study it for years.'

'But you think you've got the concentration of the inhibitor correct?' Betty asked.

'Well, yes,' Sterns replied. 'On paper, anyway. But . . . even if this goes perfectly . . . If we induce an episode and deliver exactly the right dose . . . I still can't promise this will cure Bruce. It might only be an antidote to suppress the specific flare-up.' He peered at Bruce. 'When you have one of these 'spikes', is the experience . . . extreme?'

'You might say that,' Bruce deadpanned.

'I can't wait to see it!' Sterns chirped. His expression grew serious. 'I'd be remiss, however, if I didn't point out that if we overshoot by even a small integer . . . These concentrations carry extraordinary levels of toxicity.'

'You mean it could kill him,' Betty translated.

'Well, yes,' Sterns agreed. 'Most definitely.'

Betty and Bruce glanced at each other. It sounded like a big decision to make, but Bruce would try anything if it meant never losing control to The Hulk again.

'There's a flip side to that,' Bruce said. 'If we miss on the low side – if we induce me and the antidote fails – it will be very dangerous for you,' he warned them.

Dr Sterns leaned back in his chair and stretched his arms behind his head. 'I've always been more curious than cautious,' he said. 'It's served me well so far. But if that's what kills this cat in the end . . . well, at least I'll have peeked round a few corners.' He clapped his hands together abruptly. 'So, then, we're agreed?'

Betty and Bruce both nodded.

'Into the glorious unknown!' Dr Sterns cheered.

Blonsky stood alone in a military-base locker room, staring at his radically changed body in the mirror. His shoulders and neck were now roped with thick muscle. He turned slightly to view his back. The bones in his spine had grown, too, and they protruded between his enlarged back muscles.

Blonsky grinned crazily at himself in the mirror.

A few hours later he boarded a high-tech helicopter with a troop of other special forces soldiers. Besides him, there were three two-man shooting teams. Thermal scopes and rifles were racked against the wall.

Blonsky sat beside a soldier who had been in the Culver University battle.

'How you feeling, man?' the soldier asked him.

'Like a monster,' Blonsky replied with a grin. He raised his arm and flexed his immense bicep. The sheer bulk of his arm muscle tore his sleeve wide open.

Sparr and Ross headed back to the troops to brief them on the mission. Sparr handed out copies of the blueprints of Sterns's Empire State University building, as well as blueprints of the surrounding buildings.

'Back on The Hulk hunt, Major!' Blonsky cheered.

'Banner is the target, Captain,' Ross reminded him.

'Snipers have the point,' Sparr instructed. 'Delta in back-up. If we get there before they move again, we'll have two tries. If we can't take him inside, we'll try for a shot as he exits. Under no circumstances is Banner to be engaged directly.'

'And if he goes nuclear?' Blonsky asked.

'He's never turned unless he was cornered or hurt,' Ross replied. 'If we can't take him out long-range, or if he runs, we fall back and *let him go*. Any other questions?'

'Not much of a rematch,' Blonsky complained.

Sparr glared at him. 'There are one-point-five million people within a five-mile radius of the target,' she snapped. 'You want to fight that thing there?'

With that, Sparr stormed towards the front of the helicopter and sat at her station.

Ross joined her. 'You sure about your boy?' Sparr asked.

Ross nodded. 'I need a dog in the hunt that's not going to run from the bear,' he explained. 'If we do this right, I'll never have to let him off the leash.'

Dr Sterns and Betty prepared Bruce's experimental procedure. Betty thought that the lab table looked disturbingly like a prison bed for administering lethal injections. The whole laboratory had a Dr Frankenstein vibe that made her feel unnerved.

Bruce stripped to his stretchy Lycra shorts and handed his clothes to Betty. 'Think of all the money I'll save on wardrobe if this works,' he joked. When she didn't laugh, his expression grew solemn. 'If this starts to go bad,' he said, 'promise me you won't try to help me.'

'Bruce –' Betty began.

'It's the worst when it starts,' he interrupted. 'You have to promise me you'll run or I can't do this.'

Betty nodded.

Dr Sterns pointed to the medical restraints on the lab table. 'If you have a strong reaction, these will keep you from hurting yourself.'

Bruce chuckled. 'If I have a strong reaction,' he replied,

'you won't need to worry about me.' He climbed up on to the table and lay down.

Dr Sterns tilted the table back, and attached the straps to Bruce's wrists and ankles. Betty helped him insert an IV linked to the cell saturation machine in each of Bruce's arms and legs. Dr Sterns opened a canister containing the antidote and connected it to a plunger attached to the IV tubes. Finally Dr Sterns stuck contact pads connected to electrical wires on to Bruce's temples.

'Ready?' the professor asked.

Before Bruce could reply, Dr Sterns pressed the switch, and Bruce was jolted with electricity. His body bucked with uncontrollable spasms, his muscles straining against straps, his eyes clenched shut.

Then Bruce's eyes snapped open, glowing with an intense green light.

The pulse of vibrant green flashed in the base of Bruce's skull, and green gamma energy coursed through his body as his skin flooded with colour.

'My goodness!' Dr Sterns blurted.

'There's more,' Betty warned.

Bruce writhed as the full force of the transformation hit him, and his muscles swelled, stretched and hardened. His bones cracked as they adjusted to his new shape.

Betty winced as Bruce howled with pain.

Sterns covered his mouth, staggered by the changes. He stepped closer.

The restraints popped, like rubber bands, around Bruce's thickening wrists. One strap slapped Dr Sterns in the face, knocking him back as The Hulk appeared on the table, still shuddering with pain.

'Now!' Betty yelled. 'Do it!'

The lab table buckled under the giant's weight. He raised his head, growling, his eyes filled with rage.

Betty jumped up on to the table and leaned against the creature's torso, staring directly into his furious green eyes. 'Bruce, stay with me!' Betty ordered.

He just roared.

'Do it now!' Betty screamed.

Finally, Dr Sterns recovered enough to hit the button. The antidote started to flow down the tubes.

For a long moment it seemed to have no effect. But then, miraculously, the process started to reverse itself! The antidote flowed through the giant's veins, calming the radiation fire in his blood. He dwindled, and eventually The Hulk was gone; all that remained was a shivering, tired Bruce.

Still kneeling above him, Betty stroked Bruce's forehead. He was drenched with sweat. 'It's all right,' Betty whispered. 'You're all right. It's over.'

After Bruce felt well enough to discuss the experiment,

Dr Sterns gave his take on how it had gone. 'Now maybe we've neutralized those cells permanently or maybe we just suppressed that event,' Sterns said rapidly. 'I'm inclined to think the latter, but it's hard to know, because none of our test subjects survived . . . but you!'

'So how did you know it would work?' Betty asked.

'I didn't,' Dr Sterns answered. 'But now that we have the data on Bruce's initial –'

'Wait,' Bruce interrupted. 'What test subjects?'

A smile lit up Dr Sterns's face as he gestured for them to follow him to the door.

Sniper teams took roof positions around the Empire State University lab building. Each team consisted of one shooter and one spotter with a thermal scanner.

In the command van nearby, Ross and Sparr watched as their monitors lit up with readouts from those scanners – thermal images of Betty, Bruce and Sterns moving through the lab.

'Target is the tallest,' Sparr told the snipers. 'Standing in the middle.'

Downstairs in the ESU Science Building, an NYPD SWAT officer hustled a chunky security guard out of the lobby, and Blonsky and his team marched into position by the elevators.

'What have you been doing?' Bruce demanded. He glared around at the racks of test-tubes, animal cages, and high-tech replication equipment in Dr Sterns's second lab.

'Well,' Dr Sterns explained cheerfully, 'you didn't send me much to work with, and I couldn't risk blowing the opportunity, so we concentrated it and grew more.'

Pure horror darkened Bruce's face – this was his worst nightmare coming true! The Hulk in his blood was now loose in these test-tubes.

'We haven't had any survivors yet, of course,' Dr Sterns chattered on, 'and we're still trying to figure out which is more toxic, your blood or the gamma, but –'

'We've got to destroy all of it,' Bruce broke in.

'Sorry, what –?' Dr Sterns spluttered.

'All of it,' Bruce insisted. 'Right now. Is this your whole supply?'

Dr Sterns gulped, and his cheerful expression vanished. 'You must be joking,' he whined. 'We'll share a Nobel Prize for this, the three of us! Think of the applications.'

Bruce shook his head firmly. 'It doesn't matter,' he said. 'You don't know the power of what we're dealing with here!'

'But we've got the antidote now!' Dr Sterns argued.

From the rooftop nearby, the snipers watched as Bruce moved in front of the window. They raised their rifles in anticipation.

Then Betty shifted in front of Bruce, blocking the clean shot.

'At your discretion, shooter,' Sparr told the snipers.

'Almost . . .' one sniper reported over the radio. 'No, no shot.'

Downstairs, Blonsky lost his patience and bolted into a stairwell.

His teammates quickly radioed Ross. 'Blonsky's going in!'

'Blonsky!' Ross ordered. 'Stand down!'

But Blonsky was jumping up the stairs with astounding leaps, running up eight flights in seconds.

'The military doesn't want the antidote!' Bruce yelled at Dr Sterns. 'They want a weapon!'

Dr Sterns waved his hands. 'Oh, I hate the government, too,' he said, 'but you're being a little paranoid, don't you think?'

Bam! A hole appeared in the windowpane behind Bruce.

Bruce's eyes suddenly glazed over. He turned to reveal a tranquillizer dart sticking out from the back of his neck.

Dr Sterns screamed.

CHAPTER 21

Bruce's knees buckled, but Betty caught him before he fell. Then Blonsky burst through the lab door, his rifle raised.

'No!' Betty screamed. She jumped in front of Bruce.

Blonsky smiled, and shoved her aside – hard. Betty flew five feet before slamming down on her arm. She cried out with pain.

Bruce's eyes flashed with anger, but they dimmed as he struggled to focus.

With a crazy laugh, Blonsky punched Banner, knocking him to the floor. He grabbed the front of Bruce's shirt and raised him off the ground with one arm. Blonsky glared into Banner's hazy eyes. 'Come on!' he shouted. 'Where is it?' He smacked Banner across the face.

When he didn't get a reaction, Blonsky cocked back his rifle butt, ready to crack Banner in the head with it.

Three more soldiers burst into the lab. 'Blonsky, stop!' one commando shouted.

'Show it to me!' Blonsky screamed at Banner, still

holding him up with one hand. When Banner didn't move, Blonsky bashed him in the head with a solid crack.

The alley behind the lab was closed off by police vehicles. The command van backed up to the pavement outside the lab, its doors open. Sparr and Ross watched as Banner, bound by enormous wrist shackles, was rolled out of the building on a gurney. There was a thick cold pack on his head where Blonsky had hit him, and amazingly he was awake but groggy. Two soldiers escorted the gurney into the back of the van.

Betty had walked out of the building with the gurney, her wrist in a splint. Lingering to consult with a military medic behind her, she let Bruce go ahead of her.

As the gurney reached Ross, he stopped it and looked down into Banner's dizzy eyes. Ross whispered, 'If you took it from me, I'll put you away for the rest of your life.'

When Betty saw her father talking to Bruce, she hurried over, and Ross quickly waved the gurney into the van.

'Betty –' Ross began.

Betty strode after the gurney, refusing to speak to the general. Ross stared blankly at her back.

'I've never seen anyone come round from a tranquillizer dose like that,' Sparr told Ross, coming up behind him. 'Why the hell aren't we keeping him under?'

'You want to be the one to stick a needle in his arm that he doesn't want?' Ross asked. 'Betty's our best insurance. Keep her right next to him. He knows if he pops off, she's the one who will get hurt.'

Sparr nodded. 'What do you want to do with Sterns?' she asked.

Ross narrowed his eyes. 'I want him pinned in that lab with you,' he replied. 'Don't let him leave until he's identified everything in the place.'

When the van reached Central Park, where the helicopter had landed, Bruce was led in shackles out of the van. He had come round enough to walk now, and soldiers marched him up the back ramp of the helicopter under Ross's watchful gaze.

Betty tried to follow Bruce, but this time Ross grabbed her arm. 'Betty –'

'I will never forgive you for what you've done to him,' Betty spat. 'And to me.'

'He is a fugitive,' Ross retorted. 'He made choices, and I have a responsibility –'

'You made him a fugitive!' Betty yelled. 'To cover your failures!'

Ross's lips pressed together in a tight line. 'His work . . .' he said, 'his blood . . . are the property of the United States Army. My duty supersedes my personal feelings.'

Betty wrenched her arm out of his grip. 'Don't speak

to me as your daughter,' she said. 'Not ever again.' Then she strode up the ramp into the helicopter.

'It's *because* you're my daughter,' Ross said to her receding figure, 'that you're not in handcuffs too.'

An army ranger stood sentry outside Dr Sterns's laboratory doors while Sparr questioned the professor. Dr Sterns sat in a chair, acting defiant in spite of his nervousness, while Sparr paced in front of him. 'Are you telling me you can make more like him?' she demanded.

'Not yet, no,' Dr Sterns replied. 'We've sorted out some of the pieces, but I don't think I could put together Humpty Dumpty just yet. Anyway, what happened to him was a freak accident – the goal is to do it better!'

Sparr nodded. 'But Banner's the only one we've got to worry about –'

She jerked suddenly, her eyes rolling. Then she slumped to the floor.

Blonsky was standing behind her. He'd just slammed her with his knife's butt.

'What is it with you hitting people?' Dr Sterns gasped.

Click! Blonsky pulled out a nasty-looking pistol, cocking it in Dr Sterns's face. 'I want what you got out of Banner.'

Dr Sterns peered at Blonsky. 'You look like you've got something extra in you already, don't you?'

Blonsky stood to his full, exaggerated height, flexing his giant muscles. 'I want more,' he said. 'You saw what he becomes?'

'I did,' Dr Sterns replied. 'It's beautiful.'

'Make me into that,' Blonsky ordered.

Dr Sterns raised his eyebrows. 'But I don't know what's already in you . . . The mix could be something terrible.'

Blonsky grabbed Dr Sterns by the front of his white jacket and yanked him out of his chair. Then he placed his gun under Dr Sterns's chin.

'I'm not unwilling,' Dr Sterns said.

Minutes later Blonsky was lying on the lab table, and Dr Sterns hooked him up to the cell-saturation machine. The professor rapidly attached a 'Mr Green' blood canister to the infusion port, and then slid the gamma machine's emitter into place.

Blonsky looked up at his reflection in the silver disc of the emitter and saw white crosshairs moving over his forehead.

The helicopter buzzed through the night sky over the Hudson River. Ross sat up front with his intelligence team while Bruce and Betty sat on benches across from each other in the rear, both flanked by soldiers.

The radio crackled.

'Sir!' cried a panicky voice.

'This is Ross,' the general replied.

'Something just took out Dr Sterns's lab,' the soldier reported. 'Blonsky and the major are still up there! Huge machinery exploded through the wall!'

'Get our guard support teams back there,' Ross ordered, 'and get PD Special Units out –'

The radio squawked with an enormous crash and a bone-chilling roar of rage.

'The Hulk is in the street!' the soldier cried into the radio.

Ross glanced down the helicopter interior at Banner, who stared back at him.

'That's impossible,' Ross said into the radio. 'Now hold it together, soldier! Have any of you got a live feed?'

'Yeah,' the soldier answered.

'Then stay with it – whatever it is – and get me a visual,' Ross said. 'We've got help on the way. Now get moving!' Ross broke off radio communication, then turned to the helicopter's pilot. 'Turn us around,' he ordered.

The helicopter banked sharply.

CHAPTER 22

The helicopter swooped towards Harlem, where explosions and commotion could already be seen from the air.

Ross stared at the video monitors as the soldier raced in a Humvee up a street parallel to the creature who was wreaking havoc. He caught a glimpse of the monster's rear flank, with smashed cars rolling behind it, but then it disappeared behind a building. It had looked Hulk-like, but the view had been too brief.

'I said get me eyes on that thing!' Ross shouted.

Bruce pushed past the soldier guarding him and joined Ross by the monitors. Betty quickly followed.

On the monitor, the Humvee had reached 125th Street. It slammed on the brakes, and the video picture lurched around. When the image settled, Ross, Bruce and Betty's jaws dropped. They could see a massive, brownish-green creature gleefully causing chaos. Pedestrians fled in panic, and cars skidded, smashing into hydrants.

'Sir, are you seeing this?' the soldier called. 'Is that

Banner?' he continued, his voice trembling.

'It's not Banner!' Ross snapped. 'Hold position!'

The monster stomped towards the Humvee, and the occupants of the helicopter got their first good look. The creature was at least fourteen feet tall and ridiculously muscled. He was as brawny as The Hulk, but he had strange bone spurs protruding along his ankles and wrists and down his spine.

The camera panned up to his snarling face – a face they all instantly recognized.

'Blonsky,' Ross said, breathlessly dismayed. 'What have you done to yourself?'

Blonsky had become an Abomination.

Bruce shook his head; his worst fears had come to life.

'Listen to me, soldier,' Ross told the commando in the Humvee. 'Hit it with whatever you've got and then run. Try to draw it after you to the river. We'll send reinforcements.'

But then a crumpled car hurtled through the air, right at the camera. A huge fireball exploded upward, and the camera fell to the ground, wobbling as it looked up at the sky. The Abomination swung into view, leering down. He raised his clawed fist high and brought it down with a thud.

The camera fuzzed out, and the monitor went black.

Bruce, Ross and Betty sat in silence.

Then the radio squawked again. 'General,' a

communications officer said, 'the NYPD want to know what to use against it. What do you want me to tell them? Sir?'

Ross stared silently at the dead monitor.

'Sir?' the communications officer prompted again over the radio.

Ross shook off his shock. 'Tell them to bring everything they've got and head for Harlem,' he ordered. He lowered his head. 'And heaven help them,' he whispered. The general's face was tired and grim – he knew the military had no way to fight the monster.

'The sound waves stopped The Hulk,' Betty suggested.

'They need an open field of fire,' Ross replied flatly. 'There's too much down there to absorb the sonic waves. There are too many places to hide.'

'You can't stop him,' Bruce said. 'You have to kill him.'

Ross let out a scary laugh. 'And what do you propose, a bomb? How big should it be – you tell me!'

Bruce didn't say anything for a long moment. 'You have to take me back there,' he said in a resigned voice.

'No!' Betty snapped.

'It's the only way,' Bruce said. '*I'm* the only thing that can stop him.'

Ross shook his head. 'Forget it. You won't fight, you'll run.'

'We made that thing, you and I!' Bruce argued. 'There are people getting hurt. We've got to try something!'

Betty wrapped her fingers around Bruce's arm. 'You think you can control him?'

'No,' Bruce admitted, 'but maybe I can *aim* him. I think you were right. I'm in there. I heard you on the table calling to me and I held on –'

'What if you just double my problem?' Ross asked.

Bruce raised his eyebrows. 'Have you got a better idea?'

Ross closed his eyes, then slowly nodded his head. 'Put us near him,' he instructed the pilot. Then he called to the soldiers in the back of the helicopter. 'Get those cuffs off Banner.'

'No, stay high,' Bruce said. 'And open the rear door.' When Ross gave him a sceptical look, Bruce barked, 'Do it!'

Ross nodded. A soldier hit a button, and the ramp of the helicopter hinged open. Cool air rushed inside.

Bruce hurried towards the rear, still locked in the wrist shackles. 'Put me over it!' he instructed. 'Go higher!'

The helicopter surged upward, and the city dropped away. Bruce peered down from the open door. New York was three thousand feet below them, glowing in the darkness. Another explosion bloomed up in Harlem, but from that height, Bruce couldn't hear the screams.

'No, what are you doing?' Betty yelled. 'You don't know if you'll turn!'

Bruce closed his eyes. 'A long time ago, when I thought

I'd killed you, I tried to stop him,' Bruce told her. He opened his eyes and met Betty's gaze. 'He wouldn't let me.'

Bruce backed up on to the ramp, which sloped precariously into the air.

Betty seized the cargo netting along the wall with one hand and grabbed Bruce by his shackles with her other. 'This is too risky!' she cried.

Bruce nodded. 'I have to try. I'm sorry.' He took a deep breath, kissed her quickly, and then pulled her hand off his shackles.

He let himself fall backwards off the ramp. The wind whooshed around him as he tumbled down towards 125th Street. He closed his eyes and let himself fall, waiting.

He fell. And fell.

Nothing happened. No burst of energy or anger or power. Nothing.

Bruce's eyes snapped open. Uh-oh, he thought.

He plunged at unbelievable speed towards the street below.

CHAPTER 23

A flash of green flared above the city, plummeting into Harlem. He crashed into the street in an explosion of asphalt and dirt, leaving a very deep, rough hole in the roadway.

Down the street, The Abomination was inflicting terrible destruction on the city, and civilians running from his path dodged the hole in the ground from all directions.

A mighty green hand and arm rose up and grabbed the hole's ragged edge, crushing the street with its grip. The Hulk emerged from the ground.

All around were police lights flashing, people running, sirens blaring, and explosions detonating in the distance. A police chopper blared its spotlight on The Abomination down the street. The Hulk staggered, unable to stand the sensory overload of a city in chaos.

But then The Hulk closed his eyes, grimacing against the madness. He strained, all his muscles flexing, and he let out a roar, shaking his head to clear it.

Now he could concentrate on his target: The Abomination – the enemy.

The Hulk stood tall, and bellowed at his adversary, his roar shaking the street.

The Abomination turned around and saw The Hulk. His grey eyes shimmered with malicious recognition.

Hurtling towards each other, the two giants collided so powerfully that the windows of the surrounding storefronts shattered. The Abomination tackled The Hulk, knocking him off his feet, and they tumbled down the street towards Broadway, ripping up the asphalt as they rolled.

They brawled in the street, then stood upright, each whaling on the other savagely, spinning out towards an intersection. The Abomination's elbow bone protrusions slashed The Hulk's skin. The Hulk's thunderous punches rattled The Abomination, staggering him back. They smashed cars with their feet as they rumbled into the intersection.

A speeding car hit the back of The Hulk's heels. He fell on to it, and the car carried him down the road, separating him from his enemy. As soon as The Hulk pulled himself off the car, he launched back at The Abomination, who had chased him down the road. The Abomination threw a blistering roundhouse punch, but The Hulk ducked under it and pounded The Abomination in the ribs. The Abomination howled in pain, then swung out a backhand, slicing The Hulk's chest with his elbow spikes and hitting him so hard that the green creature collapsed face-first on to the hood of a car.

The Abomination pounced on The Hulk's head, smashing his face deeper into the hood. Desperately The Hulk lashed out with a side kick, knocking The Abomination away. As The Hulk struggled to pull himself to his feet, he saw that the hood had been imprinted with the shape of his face.

The helicopter buzzed low over Harlem. General Ross and Betty watched the battle from the copter. Below, the giants grappled like sumo wrestlers, each trying to overpower the other. The Hulk reared his head back, and rammed his forehead into his enemy's nose.

The Abomination toppled backwards and The Hulk leaped upon him, grabbing his skull in his hands and slamming his cranium back against the street. The Abomination curled up his body and managed to get his legs under The Hulk's torso. With an ear-splitting roar, he pushed with the full force of his massive legs, blasting The Hulk backwards through the air.

From her high perch, lying on the helicopter ramp, Betty gasped as she saw The Hulk sail over a rooftop, clipping off the brick corner of an elevator shaft tower. He came down between two buildings, smashing into an apartment fire escape. The Hulk dropped into the alley and landed on a dumpster, pulverizing it.

The Abomination rumbled down the street, accelerated like a long-jumper, and soared up into the side of the first building, digging massive handholds into the bricks as he scaled the apartment.

General Ross peered down from the helicopter over the gunner's shoulder, narrowing his eyes as he saw The Abomination climbing. 'Use that weapon, soldier!' Ross ordered the gunner. 'Give him some help!'

'Which one?' the gunner asked.

'Shoot that one climbing the wall!' Ross retorted. 'Which one do you think?'

Tracer fire streaked down in the dark as the gunner blasted the helicopter's cannon down at The Abomination. Bricks exploded around the climbing creature.

The Abomination managed to reach the rooftop, where the gunner had a clearer shot. Cannon rounds streaked down at him, ripping up the roof. Some of the rounds ricocheted off The Abomination's platelike bones, but others ripped through his flesh.

The Abomination headed for a water tower, sprinting across the roof with the helicopter tight overhead. Betty clung to the helicopter's ramp as it accelerated to keep up.

Down in the alley, The Hulk heard the sound of firing

above. He shook himself off, growled, and then bounced off the close walls of the alley, scaling the space parkour-style. When he reached the top, he jumped on to the remaining fire escape and pulled himself on to the roof.

The helicopter hovered to his left, raining cannon fire down on The Abomination's back. The Abomination wrenched a steel girder out of the water tower's base and prepared to heave it at the helicopter, like a javelin. Up on the ramp, Betty's eyes widened in fear.

The Hulk sprinted across the roof towards The Abomination and made a dive at his enemy's neck. The Abomination managed to throw the girder, but his aim was knocked off, and both he and The Hulk tumbled off the roof.

The steel girder missed the helicopter's main rotor by inches . . . but clipped one of the tail rotor's blades. The machine whipped out of control.

'I can't hold it!' the pilot shouted. 'I've got to put it down!'

Betty lurched across the rear ramp, barely managing to hang on.

The falling giants missed slamming into the underside of the plummeting helicopter by inches. Inside the copter, Ross hung on to his chair, his jaw set firmly.

Betty closed her eyes.

CHAPTER 24

The creatures crashed into the Empire State University plaza, splintering marble paving stones as they rolled apart.

The helicopter spun out wildly around its main rotor, narrowly clearing the top of the university's library. It skittered into the dome of the main hall and crashed down into the plaza. Betty was hurled towards the front of the cabin as the tail rotor sheared off, and the rear ramp crumpled like a crushed can.

Nearby, The Abomination grabbed The Hulk and slammed him against a marble wall, pounding his body, like a boxer against the ropes. The Hulk clinched him to stop the pummelling, their faces inches apart, teeth bared with strain.

The Abomination raised his gigantic right forearm and pinned it against The Hulk's throat, the elbow spike driving into the flesh of The Hulk's chest, right above his thumping heart. The marble wall cracked behind The Hulk's head.

The Hulk gripped The Abomination's head to push

him back. In retaliation The Abomination hammered his knee into The Hulk's thigh. Across the plaza the shattered helicopter rolled once on to its side before coming to a stop.

Betty, bruised but alive, picked herself up in the helicopter's cabin. She saw her father pinned under his bent chair, struggling to free himself. Behind him, the pilot moaned. Betty pulled on her father's chair, trying to loosen the twisted metal.

'We're all right!' Ross shouted. 'Find a way out!'

Betty let go of the chair, but just stood there, staring at her father.

'Go!' Ross ordered. '*Go!*'

With a dismal cry, Betty scrambled to climb up to the gunner's door, which was now above her in the sideways helicopter.

As she raised her head out of the door, Betty could see sparks bursting in cascades from the shattered main rotor. She shoved herself past the unconscious gunner, struggling to climb out. At the other end of the plaza, she could see The Hulk and The Abomination battling against a far wall.

Betty grunted as she heaved herself up, but her leg got caught between the bent gun and the door frame. Her eyes flicked to the side, widening as she saw the sparks showering closer to the fuel tanks on the side of the helicopter, which were torn open and oozing pools of gasoline.

'Bruce!' Betty screamed.

The Hulk glanced over and saw Betty squirming in the wreckage.

A bright green pulse flashed at the base of The Hulk's skull. He let out a violent roar as new power surged into him, and his body rippled with additional muscles.

The Abomination's eyes grew wide as The Hulk seized his wrists and slowly spread his arms. The Hulk drove his knee up under The Abomination's ribs, and the monster doubled over. The Hulk grabbed The Abomination's back, then launched the monster head first into the marble wall.

With his enemy momentarily disabled, The Hulk sprinted for Betty as the first spark hit the fuel tank with a blinding whoosh of flame.

Halfway there, The Hulk saw that he wouldn't be able to beat the explosion. Still running, he slammed his hands together in a thunderous clap, extinguishing the flame. Betty's hair blew back in the powerful gust.

'Wow!' Betty cheered. 'Thanks!' But she gasped as she heard a crackling, rattling sound from behind The Hulk. 'Watch out!' she cried.

A tremendous blow to the side of his head bowled him over. He tried to rise, dazed, staring up at The Abomination looming above him.

The Abomination had fashioned a weapon out of a

chain running between two marble posts, and he swung it over his head like a nunchaku. The monster wound up for a second blow, his eyes glinting as he sensed victory.

The Hulk struggled to his knees, then pulled his feet under himself in a squat.

As The Abomination swung his weapon, The Hulk smashed his enormous fists into the ground to throw his enemy off balance. The force of The Hulk's fists formed a canyon in the ground.

The Abomination stumbled and slipped straight through the crack in the ground. As he fell, the chain from his weapon swung free through the air, circling The Abomination's enormous neck. The Hulk didn't hesitate. He launched himself on The Abomination and yanked the chain tightly. In a flash, the spark in The Abomination's eyes went out, and he drooped to the ground.

The Hulk had turned into a hero.

CHAPTER 25

Betty stood on the balcony of an apartment in Battery Park City, gazing out at New York Harbour. She was watching a ferry being tugged out towards the Statue of Liberty when her mobile phone rang. She pulled it out and looked at the number. With a sigh, she answered.

'Hi,' Betty said flatly.

'You're all right?' Samson asked quickly. 'When I couldn't reach you –'

'I'm not hurt,' Betty interrupted. 'A lot of people were, though.'

'I know,' Samson replied. 'It's been all over the TV. It doesn't . . . it doesn't seem real.'

'It was real,' Betty said.

Samson stayed silent for a moment. 'Come home.'

Betty ignored his words for now. 'Samson,' she asked, 'did you call somebody the night Bruce was at our home? Is that why they came for him?'

Samson gulped audibly. 'I was frightened,' he admitted.

'Please forgive me.' There was silence on the other end.

Betty closed her eyes and nodded. 'I do,' she whispered. 'But I'm not coming home yet.'

'Where are you going?' he asked, sounding alarmed.

'I have no idea,' Betty said. 'But I'll let you know when I do. I promise.'

Then she hung up.

On the balcony, Betty pulled out her digital camera and clicked to the picture of Bruce she'd taken in the truck, peering down at that sad, hopeful smile on his face.

Then she gazed out at the harbour again, trying to imagine where he was.

Hundreds of miles away, in an old, decrepit cabin somewhere in the woods, Bruce Banner strode over to a roughly made desk, and he pulled out an envelope from a drawer. Bruce opened his palm. He'd been holding Betty's mother's necklace in it tightly, and he sighed as he slid the necklace into the open envelope, addressed it to Betty, and sealed it.

EPILOGUE

Bruce sat in the lotus position in front of a pair of open doors, facing the ocean waves crashing on to the beach beyond. The breeze that wafted through the doors was salty and warm.

He slid deeper into meditation, his breathing almost unnaturally easy and even.

His new pulse monitor read forty-two beats per minute.

Bruce inhaled sharply. His pulse started to rise.

Nothing changed in the simple room, but his heart rate raced upward, reaching dangerous levels, his heart thumping strongly in his chest. He concentrated on his speeding heart until his pulse rate broke two hundred beats per minute.

Bruce's eyes snapped open. They were bright, flashing green.

His lips twitched with the tiniest hint of a smile.